MAMMOTH DAWN

MAMMOTH DAWN

Kevin J. Anderson
Gregory Benford

WordFire Press
Colorado Springs, Colorado

CONTENTS

INTRODUCTION

CLONING MAMMOTHS

In 2001, a year with great science-fictional significance if ever there was one, Gregory Benford and I were talking about *Jurassic Park* and the thrilling (but not terribly likely) possibility of resurrecting dinosaurs through modern cloning techniques. There were many reasons to believe that such a project was not scientifically feasible.

Cloning other extinct animals, however, wouldn't be so far-fetched. In fact, Greg pointed out some exploratory projects under way to take mammoth DNA recovered from well-preserved carcasses frozen in Siberia and use a modern elephant as a surrogate mother. Majestic woolly mammoths could once again walk the Earth. We found it a fascinating idea, not just for a story but it sparked our imaginations as human beings.

Especially, once we did a little research to discover that mammoths were quite likely made extinct through the actions of prehistoric man, we saw a larger story. If humans were indeed responsible for eradicating an entire species and we now had the ability to bring the species back, were we not morally obligated to do so?

And what about the dodo? The passenger pigeon, the Tasmanian tiger, and any number of other recent extinctions we had caused?

We started sending each other clippings, news articles, scientific reports. Research teams around the world were actually trying to *do* this—it seemed far more likely that we would see resurrected mammoths in our lifetimes than we would find ourselves cornered by velociraptors or T. rexes.

We wrote a novella based around the idea, "Mammoth Dawn," which was featured as the lead story in the venerable science fiction magazine *Analog* in 2002, which got considerable attention. But the idea seemed much too big to warrant only a short story. Over the next couple of years, Greg and I kept bouncing ideas back and forth, and we met several times to outline *Mammoth Dawn* as a full-blown novel. We wrote a detailed outline for the novel, chapter by chapter, adding many characters and storylines, turning this into an ambitious epic, of which the original novella would be only the first part. The outline itself ran longer than 20,000 words. Greg used his knowledge of Russian culture (he speaks the language) and even sailed up to Alaska for background flavor.

The novel of *Mammoth Dawn* would be a huge project, even for a pair of seasoned writers, entailing a great deal of travel, research, and likely years of writing. We loved the idea.

We didn't have time for it, but we meant to.

Greg and I each had other novel commitments, speaking engagements, travel obligations, and as each of us got busier and busier, *Mammoth Dawn* kept taking the back burner. Eventually, we set it aside, sure we would come back to it "someday."

A few months ago I saw a science special on TV, "How to Clone a Woolly Mammoth," that detailed the state of the current cloning efforts. Even though Greg and I had stopped working on our novel, the scientists had not abandoned their dreams. In the decade since we'd begun our plot development, research into resurrection cloning had advanced greatly.

And as expected, the controversy over the very idea had proceeded along very similar lines to what we had postulated in our story.

I looked at our materials—the original novella and our very detailed novel outline—and realized we had already written enough for a book, and we were determined to publish it before a real woolly mammoth came knocking at our door. I contacted Greg and we agreed to release *Mammoth Dawn*. He wrote a summary essay, included here, that describes the state of current work and the very real possibility that a mammoth will be appearing soon.

On the ethical issues, we believe they are best considered in the light of a close look at the imaginative possibilities—a task best done by fiction. See what you think after reading the ideas we outline here.

It's not going to be just a story for much longer.

—Kevin J. Anderson

Mammoth Dawn

The Original Novella

If only the protesters' intellect matched their verbal cleverness, Alex thought, the Helyx Corporation wouldn't have any problems at the gate.

It's Not Nice to Fool with Mother Nature! said one of the waving signs displayed on a securitycam window projected on the surface of his desk. The usual. Alex Pierce had stopped trying to understand the Evos' odd point of view, had ceased even being bemused by their antics. He had a company to run.

He relegated the securitycam image to the back-ground and brought more important documents forward. Datascreens and e-mail lists cluttered his table-sized desktop screen as much as memos and paper messages had once done.

Earlier that morning he'd woken up in Miami with a hangover. He'd downed three drinks too many at yet another fancy fund-raiser dinner—this one to preempt birth defects through parental genetic screening. Before midday he had choppered back to the main lab administration offices in rural Montana. For a worldwide corporation, business hours lasted all day long, and it was always time for the boss to get back to work.

His wife, Helen, had stayed home on the ranch. She disliked black-tie functions like the one in Miami, though she could be devastating in a cocktail dress, the barest breath of jewels implying wealth far better than gaudiness did. But too often the diplomats and VIPs treated Alex as the only important face in the room, and Helen the gorgeous trophy wife rather than a talented scientist in her own right. She hated the attitude, and Alex had made appropriate excuses for her.

But Helen's real reason was that she wanted to stay with her mammoths.

As his company had grown from a fledgling startup with one biotech product—a symbiotic microorganism that could fend off strange *E. coli* in the human digestive system—to a corporate leviathan that spent most of its resources just figuring out how to receive and manage the enormous profits, Alex had learned to multi-process. While taking care of corporate details, answering vidmessages, and delegating responsibilities, a calm and meditative part of his mind was anticipating an evening of campfires and peace with his wife, out near the herd....

"We got another fence-jumper," Ralph Duncan said on the secure phone, interrupting a dozen separate trains of thought and delivering a problem of his own. "Got him cold."

Alex's autosecretary instantly knew this was important, captured the call and transferred the Security man's weathered image to the upper corner of the desk.

"Remember that li'l hint we got on the acoustics? Tracked him in the woods up along the eastern ridgeline. Ambitious bastard."

Alex was glad to be interrupted from pharmaceutical statistics, Third World traveler health records—dull, even if they did point to continued success. "Another Evo type?"

"They don't carry some kinda ideology tag, Boss, but you can bet he was trying to get a look at the mammoths. Should I tell the sheriff?"

"No, he'll just process the guy, slap him on the wrist, and let him back out to cause more mischief." Alex rubbed his fingers over thin lips. "Usually only the hardcore ones try to get past the fences. How's he outfitted?"

"Pretty fancy. Overnight gear, one of those microbags for sleepin,' videocam with closeup fittings. Five kilometers inside the fence, easy. No question about boundaries and jurisdictions." Ralph snorted.

By now, the questions came automatically to Alex. The ranch often had intruders. "No weapon?"

"Nope. Except for tryin' to run at first, gave us no trouble."

As he dealt with the conversation, Alex finished some routine computer work, forwarded several inquiries to Helen's mailbox, bumped a set of interview questions to his PR squad (who knew all the right answers anyway), and keyed out, using his thumbprint to secure the device. At no point did Ralph ever notice that he didn't have Alex's full attention.

"If you ask me, this guy wanted to be caught. Claims he knows you professionally." Ralph's sun-grizzled face showed just a hint of amusement. "His ID says Geoffrey Kinsman."

Now Alex paid attention. "Damn! I think I know him. Spelled with a G?"

"Yep."

"What's a good biologist doing with that bunch of Luddites?"

"Says he'll talk only to you, Boss."

Alex shut down the other operations in the office, signaling all his staff distributed around the world that he was not presently available. "Bring him to the Hospital, not here."

Ralph had an intuitive sense of Alex's moods, born of a decade's close collaboration. But now the Security man seemed surprised. "Show and tell, Boss? For one of those clowns?"

"The Evos are always more afraid of what they imagine than what they actually see." He put on a pair of spex and tested the uplink as he headed out of the office, his boots clomping down the varnished wooden stairs, and out onto the plank porch. "Stall him for five, Ralph. Give me time to profile him."

When Helyx had purchased an isolated chunk of northern Montana, Alex kept the original ranch buildings, letting them fade and weather from bleached white to an ash gray like raw silver. The primary genetics labs were in the old pine-log barn, which Helen had dubbed the Pleistocene Hospital.

"Full database search," he subvocalized into the spex as he walked. "Summarize relevant information on Dr. Geoffrey Kinsman. Reference point: He was in my lab around fifteen years ago. Apply context filters."

With a big drive-in bay and concealed windows, the hospital barn looked like an equipment garage. Inside, the crisp antiseptic air mixed with the moist organic odors of feathers and fur, droppings and feed—a contrast to the smelly oil drums just outside on the loading dock.

Lounging in his jeans against the split rail that bounded the old barn, Alex read a data summary that scrolled across the spex. All he needed to know about Geoffrey Kinsman: a man with just a bit too much clout and education to dismiss as simply a misled Luddite, as Alex had always considered the Evos to be.

For years, Kinsman had associated with political activism, starting with *Ruckus Society* training camps, where bright-eyed kids learned street protest tactics. His molecular biology research had produced over a hundred papers, recently with an angle toward genetics and species preservation. Another "clean genes" guy. Unarmed, a routine lab type, Kinsman did not seem dangerous. Maybe that didn't include the threat of being bored to death.

Alex bit his lip in annoyance. He wished they had a network of sympathetic locals who would warn Helyx before a guy got this far in. He had endured the backwoods suspicions, had expected them because he'd grown up just over the Idaho border. For the first few years, the locals had given him a narrow-eyed appraisal. In fact, for a while, an ugly rumor had spread that he was here to recruit locals as organ donors for sinister Helyx experiments.

But when his staff offered only day work and some well-paid farmhand jobs, the people were disappointed—until the area economy picked up and kept growing. Within a year Alex Pierce could walk into any bar and get his beer paid for, because Helyx Ranch pumped in a goodly share of the county's revenue.

Alex pursed his lips, pondering. A lot of the locals might agree with the protester's views, even help them out a little. A bitter truth—he hadn't won the war of ideas even here, in home country. He knew these people, shared many of their gut responses. But he had not lived in their world, really lived in it, for a good long while. Ralph was the real thing—and looked it in his rough pants and boots as he came through the door with his captive.

The man walking next to him was a dapper, compact item, fresh from an upscale outfitter: olive green Gore-Tex jacket, trim all-weather leggings, a big hiker's watch with a Global Positioning readout. He looked as out of place as a chicken in church. A bit heavier than Alex remembered, but the tight mouth was the same.

Geoffrey Kinsman's voice was as hard and flat as a stove lid. "Dr. Pierce." East Coast accent, mid-Atlantic state. He held out a hand, and Alex ignored it. "You don't remember me?"

"I remember. Just read the data squirt about you, Dr. Kinsman. All the good stuff." He decided to have some fun with him. "You seem to have strayed a bit out of your way."

"Might as well admit the obvious," Ralph growled, playing the tough cop. "You wanted to create some disturbance—give the Feds a pretext to come in here."

Kinsman glanced at the old security chief as if he were some kind of lab specimen. "You overestimate my powers."

"That's just what you did at that animal experimentation facility outside Topeka, five years ago," Alex said. It sometimes put these people off balance if you could demonstrate up front that you knew all about them.

But Kinsman didn't even blink. "That was coincidence."

Ralph snorted, and Alex grinned. Kinsman was not going to be any trouble, he judged; he didn't even have a cover story. "We'll be fine, Ralph. Thank you." As the Security man turned to leave, Alex scowled back at Kinsman. "So why, exactly, was it so important to break through my fences and trespass on my private property?"

The man allowed himself a small, dry chuckle, but his eyes were a brittle gray, like chips of slate, as he said, "To talk some sense into you. I consider that constructive, not destructive."

"Sense? Those people at the South Gate have an excuse: they're ignorant. But we worked together, so I thought—"

"You didn't think twice about me when you published that paper, the one on mammoth genes."

"Right, you did some of the preliminary scans on the gene lines. A grad student for two years, then left."

Kinsman took on a self-righteous air. "I disagreed with the work, once I understood what you were doing."

"So what was your gripe? Was it because I 'didn't think twice' about you?"

"Neither of you even asked if I wanted my name on that paper."

Alex shook his head. "You were doing straightforward stuff. Not original. Sorry if we didn't acknowledge you—" He couldn't even remember for sure.

"Oh, there was a paragraph at the end, thanking me and a dozen others, sure."

Alex smiled slightly. "You wanted to be on the paper. Is that what this is about?"

"No, damn it!" But Kinsman's flushed face belied his words. "I just thought you'd listen to me because I was a lab grunt for you once. Maybe your money has insulated you from the arguments against this entire—"

Alex held up a hand, quick and decisive. "Already heard them. Before I took you on as a grad student, I had invented most of the arguments. Or my wife had. But we thought it through. Decided for ourselves."

Kinsman blinked, looking taken aback at Alex's bluntness. He must have had plenty of time to rehearse this confrontation while backpacking across Helyx wilderness property, Alex mused, but a lot of emotion churned in his face. There had been a lot of grad students in Alex's lab then, most of them doing routine tasks to get experience. Somehow this one had left little impression on him. But clearly that old, simple paper had been a big deal to Kinsman. Students normally didn't get their names on technical papers unless they did something creative, but Kinsman had apparently taken that irritating grain of sand and turned it into this pearl of a grudge. Alex had never been really good at judging people, but his years leading a stupendously successful company had sharpened what little skill he naturally had.

Nothing brings enemies out of the woodwork more effectively than success.

"Okay, let me talk some sense into *you*." Alex gestured toward the old oaks that towered near the barn and the ranch buildings. The immense, gnarled trees were majestic and stately—and full of birds. "Look over there, Dr. Kinsman. Beautiful birds, graceful. You should see them fly at sunset, like a cloud." Even without squinting, he could pick out a dozen nests in the branches, and the constant shifting, cooing, fluttering made the branches tremble.

"I didn't come here to look at birds, *Dr.* Pierce." He spat out the title.

Alex turned to him sharply. "You should. Once they blackened the skies, billions of them in North America when Columbus landed. But it was in their nature to nest in huge colonies, only in big stands of oaks or beeches, which made them easy prey. Over the centuries settlers cut down the oaks and beeches for firewood and lumber, or just to clear farmland. Hunters shot millions of those birds, usually for sport, though they shipped the carcasses to the cities by the barrelful."

Kinsman looked impatient, then startled. "Those are—"

"Passenger pigeons lay only one egg each spring. They couldn't possibly reproduce faster than they were slaughtered. It was genocide, pure and simple, *Dr.* Kinsman, perpetrated by human beings. The last passenger pigeon died in 1914 in the Cincinnati Zoo, and the species was extinct in a historical blink of an eye. Until Helyx brought them back." Alex couldn't keep the happy pride out of his voice.

Kinsman, though, looked disgusted to the point of being ill. "Extinction is Nature's way, Pierce—for whatever reason. You can congratulate yourself for the hubris of your genetic breakthroughs, but can you honestly say the world is a better place because you have brought back a ... pigeon?" He waved dismissively toward the oaks. As if at a signal, several of the birds took flight, ruby-throated, with lovely gray body feathers and long pointed tails. "Your means are dangerous, and your ends are utterly inconsequential. Pigeons!" The fire in Kinsman's eyes made Alex reconsider the wisdom of having sent his security chief away so quickly. "You're a bigshot businessman—what possible market can there be for passenger pigeons. For zoos? Pets? *Meat?*"

"Market talk is what I feed the Board, but that doesn't even start to explain why I'm here." He allowed a small, self-deprecating smile. "I didn't want to go down in history as Dr. Diarrhea." Alex turned from the split-rail fence. "Come have a look. Maybe we can use a crowbar to open your mind."

Inside, the lab was a mix of cool high-tech surfaces and ancient woods, the barn's past never wholly banished. Consoles and elaborate digital diagnostics stood next to old feed cabinets, still useful for storage. High spotlights gave the scene an evenly lighted patina and crisp, conditioned air fought the old horsey smells and new disinfectants. Chrome countertops sat next to wooden fences and thick wire-mesh cages.

"Not many people get to see this, Dr. Kinsman," Alex said.

"Not many people should."

Why do I try? he thought. *If Kinsman wasn't a colleague …*

Inside a shoulder-high pen stood two gawky-looking birds like giant chickens with stretched necks. They had mottled brown feathers, lizard-like feet, and towered nearly ten feet tall.

"This is our first mating pair of moas, a New Zealand bird that went extinct sometime in the 1600s." Elated notes crept into Alex's voice, but he saw no wonder in Kinsman's eyes. "We're currently in our third-generation retrograde development of the Tasmanian tiger, too. But the lack of a close sibling-species as well as general difficulties in dealing with the marsupial gestation process has caused some delays."

He glanced toward the set of thick doors and reinforced windows at the back of the Pleistocene Hospital. Kinsman looked suspiciously at the closed-off rooms … but Alex didn't think the man was ready for that sight yet. "Other resurrected animals," he explained with an offhanded comment. "Look, I don't have time to show you everything. It's obvious you're more interested in proselytizing than in science."

A rotund bird higher than a man's knee waddled across the floor, looking comical, its black beak blunt and ugly, its eyes innocent. Two stubby wings betrayed the flightless nature of the bird, which moved at a rapid, though ungainly clip. A tufted curlicue of feathers poked up like a pigtail from its rear. The bird prodded around in corners, pecked at imaginary insects, as if it had forgotten where its food dish was.

This time Kinsman stared. "*Dodos*, too?" The dapper man leaned forward and took out his pen, pointing it at Alex as if it were a symphony conductor's baton. "Where will you stop, Pierce? Do you intend to bring back smallpox as well? Or any number of vermin the world is better off without? Have you no respect for the natural order?"

Alex picked the ungainly bird up and carried it squawking to a bowl of grain. The dodo immediately forgot its annoyance and began to gobble the corn. "These birds lived quite nicely on the island of Mauritius until European sailors came and killed them for food. That wasn't so bad, but the sailors also let loose dogs, rats, and hogs, which ate the dodo's eggs. It took only a century or two for the entire species to be wiped out." He scratched the feathers on the turkey-sized bird. "What, exactly, is *natural* about that?"

Kinsman directed a condescending look at Alex Pierce—who captained a gigantic corporation, who had developed a cure for the digestive misery of billions—as if he were an ill-educated child. "You can't possibly predict the long-term consequences of your tampering. Forced breeding, gene-selection, wombs implanted with embryos they were never meant to carry. Why must you *push* things so much?"

"Because I don't have time to waste," Alex said mildly. "Evolution can meander all it likes. We have calendars."

Kinsman sniffed, clicked his pen twice in a nervous gesture. "Mankind is part of the natural order, Pierce, the dominant species on Earth, while other species failed along the way."

"Sometimes with a little help from us. What's wrong with rectifying that?"

Kinsman tossed his pen onto a cluttered desk and actually clasped his hands together in a melodramatic beseeching gesture. "What makes extinction caused by human interference so different from extinction due to, say, a huge asteroid impact? Will you try to bring back dinosaurs next?" He scoffed. "Or woolly *mammoths*? I've heard what you have back in your valleys."

Alex maintained a noncommittal expression. "Rumors."

"Satellite photos."

Alex didn't respond, trying to hide his surprise that Kinsman and his protesters could have gotten such high-resolution images from the Feds.

Kinsman pressed his advantage. "I want to see them, Pierce."

✦   ✦   ✦

Blocked from view by a thick stand of Ponderosa pines, the corral had once been used for breaking horses. But Helyx had reinforced the fences, added motion detectors and voltage zappers, and made the barricades much taller. As needed.

Inside the enclosure, Helen studied two of the first-generation hybrids, giving each one a standard monthly physical exam. Maybe Kinsman would be satisfied with this.

When she saw her husband pass through the double gate, Helen's face lit up. They had spoken via earlink after he'd arrived back from Miami, but both of them had been too absorbed with ranch duties to see each other before now. They would have plenty of time tonight, camping out under the stars, back where no one could find them.…

Helen rang the old notes in him with a little breath, a flash of a smile. He had called those eyes "molasses brown" because when he looked into them he felt stuck and never wanted to look away. High cheekbones, luxuriant brown hair, a delicious set of curves artfully set off in a blue blouse atop trim black jeans. She greeted Alex with a broad smile, but when she saw Kinsman follow him into the corral, she immediately adopted a more businesslike expression.

"Helen, this is Geoffrey Kinsman. Remember, he was a grad student back—"

"Oh yes. And now a member of our loyal opposition." Her voice was neutral, neither friendly nor antagonistic.

"I came to see your mammoths. I didn't know whether I could believe the appalling—"

Helen immediately clued herself in with just a glance at her husband. "Actually, these are 'mammophants.' Just a first-generation hybrid, still far from being an actual mammoth, Mr. Kinsman."

"Please, it's *Doctor* Kinsman. I got my degree at—"

"This one is Short Stuff," she continued without the slightest hesitation and stepped close to the oldest of the mixed-breeds, a docile gray-haired beast with rumpled skin and big eyes, a trunk shortened to a few feet, and no tail. "We used mammoth DNA from Siberia, inserted it into a female elephant's egg, and let the mother bring the baby to term with a lot of uterine monitoring."

Playfully, Helen reached up and slapped Short Stuff's rump, and the tall beast ambled a few feet, then stopped to munch from a pile of sage-green hay piled near a corrugated water trough. "And she's a sweetie."

Alex knew the details, had lived with them for a decade. Short Stuff was not a pure mammoth because she had spent twenty-two months in an Asian elephant's womb, sharing the chemical and hormonal bath evolved for elephants alone. But the womb had proved similar enough to a mammoth's, or the hybrid would have spontaneously aborted.

"We're learning the hard way that there's a critical conversation between the genes and the womb," Helen said. "Call it feminine knowledge. So we're still working to get the right dialog between the mammoth genes and the wombs of each new generation."

Indeed, Short Stuff's womb had turned out to be a much better approximation, and using the sperm of the first male, Middle Man, their offspring was even closer.

"You can sure see the original elephant genes showing through." Helen lifted Short Stuff's leathery left ear, as big as a blanket. "No woolly mammoth had this large an ear. It would lose too much heat in an Ice Age climate. Most of Short Stuff's body was designed for the tropics—she's got a hide that stands up under strong sun. Still, you can see the beginnings of hair, an extra coat to keep her warm. A step in the right direction."

She talked faster as Kinsman's frowning displeasure became more obvious. Helen moved to the other big animal in the corral, the first hybrid male. He snorted, curled his trunk, but she fearlessly thrust a hand into the sparse pelt beneath the massive mouth to reveal stubby, gray-brown shafts. "See Middle Man's tusks? Pretty short for now, but they'll grow longer than any elephant's."

Helen rubbed her hands along Middle Man's midsection, eliciting a pleased sort of grunt.

Kinsman ground his teeth—the first time Alex had ever seen anyone do that, outside of movies. "And what is the point of this nonsense animal? The pure species died out long ago, and your interbreeding process creates only a succession of polyglot monstrosities."

Helen gave him her patented I-don't-suffer-fools-gladly expression. "Exactly. Did you think species just jumped in one shot to a completely different form? That's why it's called *evolution*."

Kinsman eyed the two hairy elephants in the corral. "Evolution didn't make these forms—"

"Right. We did," Helen shot back. "Unlike evolution, we have a goal. Short Stuff and Middle Man are investments for the next generation."

Alex smiled; his wife was a better debater than he could ever be. And she wasn't giving away anything technical, either, trying to swamp Kinsman with pizzazz.

He did not need to know how far the plan had already progressed.

Mammoth DNA was a heritage that belonged to all humanity—paid for with private money, part of the fortune Alex had earned as "Dr. Diarrhea." Early on, before he'd learned to keep quiet about Helyx's activities here, he and Helen had published a joint paper—the one Kinsman had done some routine lab work on—showing that the difference between elephants and mammoths was only a few dozen critical loci. The media speculation *that* provoked taught them to keep their work quiet. Every journalist could see the potential, write a quick deep-think piece. But making the project happen was a career.

"You frighten me," Kinsman said, looking from Helen to Alex. "Both of you. Our environment is a vast and complicated system that adapts to changes through delicate checks and balances. Dodos and passenger pigeons and moas—and, yes, mammoths—were removed from Earth's equation long ago, and your meddling may well throw everything out of balance again."

"That's an awfully sophisticated argument for a bunch of protesters who usually can't come up with anything more pithy than 'It's not nice to fool with Mother Nature.'"

Kinsman dismissed his cohorts down at the South Gate. "They're just afraid of genetic engineering on general principles. They don't need any deeper argument than that."

"No, I don't suppose they do. People like that have always used their ignorance as a weapon." *And often it turned to violence.*

Kinsman backed toward the gate, as if afraid to get any closer to the gentle hybrids. "Your work is immoral, even aside from the ethical issues. Introducing a big grazer into lands that cows and sheep have already depleted is sure to have a major impact on the environment."

"Helyx's track record speaks for itself. We're concerned about the environment—and it isn't just corporate bullshit either," Alex said with a sigh. Whatever hope he had harbored that a real biologist would be open to rational ideas, faded as Kinsman's sour scowl deepened.

As a last shot, the man said, "You have to know that a lot of us in this world think what you're doing here is, at the very least, ugly." He flicked a disapproving glance at the furry mammophants wandering around the enclosure.

Alex could tell the discussion was over, and he knew Helen was already close to losing her cool. "I could tell you things—*ugly* things—that'd make your ears curl up in self-defense."

He remembered news images dating all the way back to the late Twentieth Century: Eco-terrorists burning fields of modified rice that would have grown in the alkaline soil and brackish water of the poorest Third World countries. Or ripping up experimental plantings of frost-resistant strawberries, like children throwing a tantrum. Later, assassinating a researcher who was developing a protozoan symbiote that would have enabled starving populations to break down cellulose and digest some forms of grass.

And if they were caught afterward, the violent protesters always seemed smug and self-justified! Thick-headed fools …

All of those things would have helped the human population, fed millions, improved the quality of life worldwide. And yet the rowdy rabble felt they were in a better position to decide what was best for the world than all the blue-ribbon panels of experts and all the United Nations committees. Yes, indeed, they sure seemed to have the best interests of humanity uppermost in their minds.

He pointedly nudged Kinsman through the gates of the corral before Helen could lash out at him, then used the direct-connect uplink in his spex to summon Ralph and a Security escort. "It's time for you to go. You've had your say … I just wish you'd had your 'listen.'"

When they emerged from the dense pines around the corral, Ralph was already there to take him away.

It wasn't until later that Alex discovered Kinsman had left his pen behind inside the Pleistocene Hospital. Rather than hurrying to give it back to the educated Luddite—was that an oxymoron?—he tossed it into a desk drawer in disgust. He had better things to look forward to that evening.

Alex rode his strong black gelding uphill, stretching himself and enjoying the zest of at last getting away from the office, far away, with Helen and the young ranch hand Cassie Worth. Clement Valley was about as deep in the wilderness as he could go and still remain on his vast acreage.

After the irksome arguments and corporate busyness of the afternoon, this was heaven. He had spurned the convenience of using a company jeep; taking the horses felt more natural, more *real*. As the dense alders and ponderosa pines closed around the narrowing four-wheel-drive road, they rapidly left the log-cabin lab buildings and the Pleistocene Hospital behind.

Cassie, the spunky and at times incredibly earnest young ranch hand, urged her horse into a trot ahead, anxious to get to the high overlook into the next valley. The young woman's long chestnut hair had been quickly woven into a thick practical braid that dangled beneath her white cowboy hat. Her face still retained a splash of youthful freckles, and her clear blue eyes held a fresh sense of wonder.

With good reason, he thought, *since she has seen miracles.*

But Alex and Helen did not hurry. Feeling anticipation build, they rode side by side, smelling the creaking saddles, the sweating horses, and the sweet sun-warmed pine sap. It had been a long time since they'd been so calm, though young Cassie's presence would dampen any amorous impulses in the sleeping bags out by the campfire. No matter; it was good just to be together.

While Helen watched approvingly, he had made a brave show of switching off his pager, but within half an hour the cloying weight of corporate responsibility forced him to turn it back on. When Helen wasn't looking, of course …

Horse Valley was more lush now than it had been for millennia. Using Helyx profits, Alex had started this ranch by channeling mountain streams into the headlands above, so that his experts could use the moisture to grow the sedges that normally flourished only in tundra. Reflections of aspen shimmered in mirror puddles of water as he headed up the slope, relishing the crisp air. Purple poets always talked about the "forest primeval" and Alex couldn't get the phrase out of his mind. *That's how this is supposed to be.*

In low-lying swampy areas beside the path, giant ferns like horned and scaly monkeys' tails curled up, flourishing next to fluted flat-leaved hyacinth—ancient plants that had not grown naturally since the last ice age. As they rode past, he sniffed the mulchy smell, wondering if the resurrected plants were edible, if there might be a high-end niche market for, say, Jurassic Salads....

"Majestica is looking ready to deliver," Cassie called over her shoulder, slowing her mare so her two bosses could catch up. "I've gotten close enough three times in the last week to take readings, but Bullwinkle doesn't like it."

Alex smiled. "They trust you, Cassie." Forget the scientists and the so-called professional handlers; this young woman had a better knack with the big beasts than anyone else on the ranch.

Helen drew a deep, satisfied breath. "It'll be our first pureblood, after fifteen years."

"Think of it as an anniversary present," he said. "Without your grandiose dreams I would have spent all my research money on a cure for flatulence." The three horses splashed across a stream, climbing steadily now.

Helen laughed. "I still think you deserve the Nobel Prize."

"Relieving the world's diarrhea problems through genetic engineering makes one fabulously rich, but earns no professional respect whatsoever."

Behind them, the view was stunning, a full mile of untouched wilderness. It felt odd to know that he owned very nearly everything within view, even from the highest vantage. Only in Montana was there enough land to tackle the really big projects that made his wife happy.

"After this, Alex, nobody will even bother remembering all the little things you did in your reckless youth."

Impatient with the two romantics, and smiling with anticipation, Cassie led them toward the top of the ridge. All around the valley, thick pine and aspen forests covered the hills. Cassie slowed her horse as they entered a rank of thoroughly stripped trees that showed long scraped gouges in the bark.

Helen was amazed, and concerned. "They're foraging all the way up here? They shouldn't be wandering so far afield." She urged her gray mare into the great field of sedges and sages so carefully arranged by innumerable days of gardening.

Cassie cocked her hat back with a wry smile. "Do you want to be the one to tell them where they can and can't go, ma'am?"

Alex made a mental note to see about putting a few sonic "discouragers" up here. He couldn't imagine what would happen if a stray happened to wander down the valley to within view of the protesters at the gate. Then he'd have to deal with the local sheriff, the Feds, a dozen regulatory agencies, and a host of tabloids....

As they emerged from the aspens, the girl's sweeping arm drew Alex's attention to the grassy lowland in the bowl of the valley. "See, they always come together at dusk. It's the best time to watch."

Their horses standing close together, the three of them looked down onto Clement Valley in the last light of afternoon. Helen could barely tear her dark eyes from the sight below, but she gave her husband a loving glance that said, *We did this, you and I.*

Alex stood transfixed by the slowly moving shapes before him. His company had been right to keep the media resolutely away from the valley, and here was the proof. You had to see the woolly mammoths for yourself.

Whenever he had a fresh glance at the herd, the beasts seemed like sailing ships. There was a stately glide to their passage as the great russet vessels crossed the flatness, each beast moving as though before steady winds. Only slowly did the mammoths tack and turn, ponderous yet inevitable.

As if Cassie had trained them to recognize her, the nearest behemoth raised its head and let out a long, soaring salute. The next took up the sound, and the next, and soon nearly three dozen massive beasts joined in the trumpeting call.

Alex felt an eerie shiver travel down the length of his spine. The strange, echoing song reached even deeper into his primal core, building in layer after layer, delving into bass notes seldom heard outside the cathedrals of Europe. Even when the haunting chorus faded into the soft sigh of a breeze among the shadowed pines, the three human interlopers remained still, afraid to move as if they had been the ones transported through time, not the mammoths.

"Humans haven't heard that call in ten thousand years," Helen said as she leaned over to kiss him. He was too overwhelmed to say anything at all.

With Cassie in the lead, sitting high on her roan mare, Alex and Helen rode down toward the mammoths in the last light of afternoon. The herd was accustomed to horses, and especially to the smell of the young ranch hand who tended them. Raised entirely without predators, the mammoths were unwary. Though his mare seemed a bit skittish, Alex did not feel threatened as he approached the magnificent woolly behemoths.

The sedge grasses were tall and resilient, grazed short and trampled flat especially around the muck of watering holes. Playing the Helyx CEO, Alex noted that at the grassy margins the cottonwood branches and even bitterbrush were being browsed down to nubs. He would have to speak to the tenders about keeping the food supply going so the animals didn't wander into the stands of trees bounding the meadows. Soon, the herd would outgrow this valley.

He made a mental note to look into buying even more land, maybe expanding the huge Helyx Ranch into adjacent valleys. The politics of doing that would be far worse than the economics; the perpetual gang of Evo demonstrators at the South Gate would grow, joined by garden-variety environmentalists. Folks around here didn't look much to the future—or to the distant past, either, it seemed—and they didn't like change....

With the approach of the horses, the mammoths snorted and stirred. Bullwinkle, the big leader of the herd, hung his shaggy head and lowered long tusks as he gazed at the others. The mixed-bag of hairy elephants had a range of body types, each generation only a few years separated from the previous, and each one significantly woollier than either of the two hybrid mammophants Alex had allowed Geoffrey Kinsman to see.

Cassie halted her mare beside a tree completely stripped of leaves and half of its bark. "Best to tie up our horses here." She dismounted with the springy grace of a gymnast. "I prefer to walk among them."

"Aren't you afraid of getting stepped on?" Helen asked.

The ranch hand flipped her braid back between her shoulder blades and adjusted her hat. "No, ma'am. But I'm afraid for the horses."

The few stands of valley grass darkened to jade as the sun settled on the distant blue mountains. A nighthawk flitted with thin cries above the willows of a narrow creek that meandered through the meadow. Alex's eyes followed the hawk up toward the peaks that towered against a hard cobalt sky already dotted with the fires of far suns. The light would fade fast, dark scarcely an hour away.

A perfect night to camp.

Cassie started ahead, glancing over her shoulder and resisting the impulse to leave the other two behind. Alex remembered when he had been that impatient, and that young—not so long ago. Though this entire project had sprung from his wife's dream decades ago, Cassie Worth was the unrelenting factotum who supercharged the Helyx staff and never seemed to sleep. She ran down innumerable practical details about exotic animal husbandry, and she figured out the answers for herself when no alleged "expert" had a clue.

Alex reflected as he watched the young woman move swiftly through the herd. To think that she had just applied to Helyx out of the blue. No advanced degrees, just solid experience at UC Davis, a farm upbringing, and an ache to bring back to the world something long gone. Alex had noted more common sense in Cassie than in half of his own VPs and Division Heads. And she had a real rapport with the animals.

"Come on you guys, I want to show them off, but I'll need to get us back up on the slope where I can set up camp for the night ... or did you change your minds again?" She turned her clear blue eyes to Alex—did he see a girlish crush there? He was abashedly reminded that he had canceled their plans three previous times for the usual "business reasons."

"Nothing's more important tonight." Alex reached over to stroke Helen's shoulder. "My wife and I are going to sleep out under the stars."

"Where I can hear my mammoths snore," Helen added.

They moved among the gigantic but gentle animals; it seemed to Alex as if he had wandered into a truck stop filled with living, hairy semis. The heavy air was laden with smells like hot oiled leather, old upholstery, musk and fur—stronger than the closeness of bison or penned cattle. But it was a wild musk, from thick and wiry hair grown to protect the beasts from the cold of an Ice Age.

Alex felt giddy.

It was a pure joy to watch Cassie in her element, like a child at a petting zoo. She led them from one large bulk to the next. Alex had never before seen so many of the beasts together in the valley. In a single glance he could see that each successive generation had fewer of the humped backs of African elephants. Instead, the younger hybrids' backs sloped down, the rich cinnamon-colored pelts thickened, and the males' tusks grew.

Closer and closer.

Cassie reached beneath the coat of the nearest hybrid and pulled up the coarse guard hair to reveal silky red under-wool. "It's so good now we should be able to leave them out all through next winter."

"Even in Montana's worst?" Alex asked, trying not to sound as if he was just protecting his investment.

"They'll love it," Helen said, smiling at the young woman.

"And they're getting interested in mating with each other now!" Cassie said, then lowered her voice as if embarrassed. "I follow them on the vidcams, and they really go at it. Just frisky play, so far. After all, they haven't reached adolescence yet. But the males are starting to herd the females—another sure sign."

Helen said softly, "We can't actually let them mate, though."

Cassie cried, "Why not? Just think—no more egg transfers, no sperm-sucking games to play." Her face wrinkled in disgust, and Alex didn't want to imagine the details of the mammophant sperm-harvesting operations.

Helen put an arm around Cassie. "We're careful with their genes. Select for mammoth aspects, weed out the elephant ones. Unchecked mating would scramble all that."

Cassie looked stricken. Plainly this had been her big announcement.

"But you're right," Helen hastily added. "Just like in nature. Desire is the only sure diagnostic." She gave her husband a quick, sultry glance. His breath caught. "These animals know, right down in their hearts—which by the way are bigger than a human head, bigger even than Alex's!—that they are worth making more of."

He hugged her. "And so we'll make more." *Some people buy diamonds for their wives ... I clone mammoths.*

Cassie made quick jabs at nearby shapes, showing off as she quickly recited the names of the other hybrids. "Those two are Rachel and Napoleon—the shorter ones are always the worst—and Angel Pie."

Alex was amazed she could identify the individual herd members so easily. The Helyx geneticists had used five to ten elephants for each step of the process, because it took twelve years for any one of the hybrids to mature to fertility. And some interbreeding attempts spontaneously aborted, Nature's editing.

Cassie led them unerringly to a huffing female, her big eyes casting a calm gaze down at the small humans. Long breaths steamed in the cooling air as dew condensed on the rocks and trampled grass. "Here, Majestica is at term and already showing signs of labor. Everything's normal, as far as I can tell. She's been in labor for about a week already."

"I can't imagine being in labor for a week," Helen said.

And the big female's gestation period had already taken nearly two years. "Mammoths and elephants aren't in much of a hurry about these things," Alex said.

Actually, the gestation period had varied with each hybrid generation, as the offspring approached pure mammoth stock. According to her continuing researches into the original genome, using numerous fourth-order projections with hypercomputers inside the pine-walled stable building, Helen was convinced that the mammoth gestation time in the Pleistocene would have been longer than a modern elephant's twenty-two months. One of the earlier female hybrids, Alexandria, had carried her baby for twenty-three months.

"We're converging toward the mammoth pattern in the ancient wild, I bet," Helen said.

Alex smiled wryly. Given her anxious attention to all aspects of the projects, his wife probably would have preferred to keep the pregnant Majestica in a separate corral back at the Pleistocene Hospital, with a whole bank of real-time blood-test gear, round-the-clock technicians, and a full array of instrumentation and diagnostics surrounding her pregnant bulk.

However, these creatures needed to bear their young naturally, in the wild, and Cassie Worth had seen more live births among ranch stock than any of Helyx's experts. She was ready.

But no one alive had ever seen the birth of a real woolly mammoth.

The smoke of green branches and dry wood wafted up from the campfire, crackling with a pungent, sweet bitterness. Alex breathed deeply, smelling the heady primal scent. Hidden in the gathering darkness, insects and night birds set up a simmering background music that seemed to come from a different time altogether.

Below them in the valley, under the light of the waxing moon and a billion stars in transparent Montana air, the herd of elephant-mammoth hybrids settled down for the night. Many of the big dark shapes still moved about restlessly. While some slept like mounds of dirt near the watering hole, others paced around, munching on sedge grass. Eerily, some of the mammoths on the fringe looked as if they were keeping watch.

Cassie busied herself, happy to be out camping, much more comfortable here within sight of her mammoths than up around the administration buildings. She never tried to understand the protesters, preferring to ignore them by staying far from the gate. "People always find something to complain about, especially when somebody else is successful," she had said once.

The young woman had outdone herself with the fire, the bedrolls, the childishly simple dinner of hot dogs roasted on twigs over the flames, a speckled blue-enamel coffee pot hung over the coals. All they needed was marshmallows (and Alex wouldn't have been surprised if Cassie had them stashed in her saddlebags). A perfect evening, in every detail.

Helyx could have provided the most sophisticated camp equipment, thermal chargers for foodpacks, heated sleeping bags and damp-resistant tents. Alex could have assigned workers to set up comfort-weave tents, groom the clearing, erect tables, string lanterns, even prepare a gourmet meal.

But this was better, much better.

"When do we start singing 'Kum-bay-ya'?" Alex said with a grin to his wife.

"I have a strummerpack," she answered, calling his bluff.

Alex's implanted pager tingled, and he recognized the source. He reached up, touching a contact point. "What's the trouble, Ralph?"

Helen frowned at him, mouthed the words, *I thought you turned that off?*

"Can't figure, Boss." His usually casual voice now sounded pinched with concern. "We're getting pinged by microwaves. Somebody's interrogating a passive receiver. Must be located somewhere around the ranch buildings."

"Not one of ours?"

"No chance. Just a simple incoming pulse from some airplane, flying pretty high. Don't think anybody could get much from that, maybe just a location marker. The pulse could be hitting some tiny receiver that shoots it back with a li'l information attached, I'd guess. Not powerful enough for us to track down where it is, though."

"Probably some new gear brought in by the demonstrators at the gate," Alex suggested. He didn't need a new technical puzzle to ruin his jealously planned evening.

"Could be, Boss. Those Evo types have plenty to spend on new toys."

"Keep on it." He disengaged the pagerlink, saw both Cassie and Helen staring at him with concern. He made a placating gesture but didn't volunteer any details. The ranch hand would assume it was yet another corporate emergency such as had canceled their first three outings; Helen, though, could read his expression much better. Her molasses-brown eyes trapped him again, looking like bottomless wells in the smoky campfire shadows.

He leaned against Helen as they both stared into the throbbing orange and yellow embers. Their clothes smelled of sweat mixed with the musk of mammoths. Alex preferred this sharp but resonant aroma to the infrequent, expensive perfumes his wife felt obligated to wear at ecological fundraisers—like the recent one she'd skipped in Miami.

Under the stars, Alex helped with the bedding down chores, glad for the chance to get his hands dirty rather than just pound on a computer keyboard all day. It felt good, and safe, to be out here, "just like a real person."

The crackling wood made him think of the prehistoric hunters, Cro-Magnon warriors who had tracked herds like this using spears and pits and cliffs to kill the giant animals for food, fur, and ivory.

Like the restored bison on the Great Plains, Helen's dream-experiment might turn out to be so wildly successful that large numbers of these once-extinct creatures could roam the open Montana range. They might wander north into Saskatchewan and Alberta, heading up toward the subarctic regions for which their huge bodies were designed.

He had been so focused on working one generation after another, converging toward a full-blood woolly mammoth, that he had not let his mind wander far into future possibilities.

"Maybe one day we'll have a large herd of mammoths that breed true and reproduce in the wild." He ran fingers over Helen's hair, recalling Kinsman's concern (one of his few legitimate ones) about the impact a sizable group of such huge grazers would have on the landscape and environment. What if they had to thin the herd? "Can you imagine if we had enough of them that we could even sponsor a good old-fashioned mammoth hunt?"

Cassie, very protective of the animals, glared across the fire at him. "What! Use guns on my mammoths?" She had been working here only two years, but the mammoths were *hers*. "Not unless you play fair." The girl's firm lips curled into a devilish grin on her freckled face. "Dress your big-game hunters in furs, then send them out with stone axes and sapling spears. Pleistocene rules. I don't think you'd get many takers."

"Not me," Helen said. "Not for all the testosterone in the world."

Alex returned a noncommittal smile. He did not argue, but he knew both women were wrong. Over the years, he had encountered any number of too rich, too bored, dot-com millionaires or genetics patent holders—people who had delusions of immortality and an overblown sense of necessary machismo.

Even with Pleistocene rules, Alex knew he could find plenty of takers....

✦　　✦　　✦

As he bedded down next to Helen, the moon continued to rise, spilling silver light. Even here, as isolated as one could be in the continental U.S., he felt as if he were under a spotlight. He couldn't sleep, and he knew Helen was awake and thinking beside him.

Below, the mammoths sounded restless. Snuffles and loud snorts rippled through the big animals. Most of them seemed awake. On the other side of the fire, young Cassie sat alone, her knees drawn up to her chin as she stared down into the valley, reflecting the animals' uneasiness.

Alex couldn't imagine what possible threats or predators could worry the gigantic prehistoric beasts this deep within ranch property. "Are they like this every night?"

Impishly, Cassie raised her eyebrows. "I *do* have quarters of my own back in the complex, Dr. Pierce. Sleeping outdoors is a treat for me, too."

A bright meteor streaked overhead, low and horizontal, like a rocket on the Fourth of July. It came over the line of trees on the ridge, flying hot, traveling with a speed and deadly accuracy that surpassed any shooting star.

Make a wish …

Helen was already on her feet, leaping out of the blankets on the damp ground. "It's heading toward the lab complex!"

The trail of fire faded into orange against midnight blue, and the incandescent arrow struck the valley behind them with a bright flash. The main Helyx compound. A muffled *whump*.

As Alex lurched to his feet, the implanted pager tingled again. "Boss, we've been hit down here. Somebody sent in a mini-cruise, I'd say. Hit the pines close to the Hospital … still trying to assess the damage."

"A mini-what?" Alex subvocalized, and his words went back to Ralph.

"Backpack-sized cruise missile, Boss. Short-range, with a nose full of high explosive. A man can carry one a fair way, then launch it from a rack."

Helen was already racing for her horse while Alex paused to get an update. "I'm going there!" she shouted and swung herself up bareback. "Short Stuff and Middle Man are still in the corral."

"Wait! You can't do anything—"

"Just work things out with Ralph," she called over her shoulder, then raced her horse down the four-wheel-drive road and disappeared into the shadowed trees. He had never seen her ride like that before.

Reacting on instinct, Cassie was at their supply packs. She withdrew the two shotguns she had carried with them, ostensibly for protection against coyotes or bears.

Alex didn't need to think hard about who might have done such a thing. "Kinsman was a decoy," he said to Ralph. "Him and his supposedly reasonable discussion, he was just a plant to get inside. But how could they target the hospital in the dark and from so far away?"

"I'm willing to bet they targeted this place with those microwave echoes I keep hearing. If Kinsman planted some sort of passive echo locator—"

"His pen! Damn, I didn't even think! He left it on purpose. They could have targeted from that. I'm packing up Cassie, and we'll be right down there."

Before Alex could switch off, the Security chief said, "Wait—that's gunfire. Jesus, those bastards are coming in from the South Gate!" Ralph's voice strayed for a moment as he barked orders to a security crew, who scrambled in response. "The Hospital's in flames, Boss. We're sending people in to try and rescue the animals."

"Keep yourself safe," Alex barked. "Helen's already on her way." He thought of the two adult mammophants in the corral, the wonderful dodos and moas, all the exotic and frightening animals he kept in the solid-wall pens in the back of the Hospital. And all of his people. He prayed his wife would be safer down there with Ralph and his crew than up here. "We're coming in—"

Another thin patter of popgun shots rang out. Alex thought he was getting Ralph's background noise until Cassie cried, "Just below us!"

"Ralph, we've got intruders up here, too."

"Clement Valley! Jesus, do you want me to send a—"

"You just do your job there. And watch Helen's back, dammit."

He shut down his link and studied the shadowy trees. Another few shots, yes, nearby. One of the mammoths bellowed in surprise, or perhaps pain, sounding like a squeaky cannon.

"Hey!" Cassie tossed Alex one of the shotguns, and he caught it instinctively. The weapon felt hard and cold and strange in his hand. She looked at him with an anguished face. "Maybe that missile hitting the Hospital was just to get our forces away—so they could come up here and kill my mammoths." She swung herself up onto her already frightened mare and bent low, snatching the tether rope. "I'm going down to the herd."

The gunshots came faster as she rode hard down into the valley.

"Wait!" Alex called after her—pointlessly—then got his butt in gear.

He mounted his own gelding and followed her into the darkness. Here he was, the head of a gigantic international corporation—and his wife and a young girl had both jumped into action while he stood around and talked to himself.

The horses were already uneasy with the smell of the mammoths, and the pattering gunfire spooked his mount even more. He caught up to the young ranch hand as she tried to see down into the darkness. "You leave the mammoths alone!"

"Quiet!" he urged, fearing the shadowy attackers might target Cassie instead of the animals.

Sharp, flat shots from their left.

Alex saw dim shapes running, stalking closer, as if intimidated by coming so close to the prehistoric beasts. Simple rifles would have little effect on a woolly mammoth, he thought—just before another round of muffled percussive bangs.

A few seconds, then distant explosions came from the open valley floor.

"Grenade launchers."

"You bastards!" Cassie screamed.

"Hush! They don't know we're up here." He and the young ranch hand were still on a slope above the trees, a hundred meters from the open grassland. They urged their horses closer. It was quiet for a moment, a deathly stillness.

The mammoths churned about, grunting, drawing closer like covered wagons circling against a Comanche attack. Amazingly, acting on instinct, the bigger bulls formed outer ranks, clearly to protect the rest of the herd. The alpha male, Bullwinkle, with its huge tusks and russet fur, snorted and moved forward like a locomotive, looking for an enemy.

No sign of the shadowy figures, but the fringe forests offered plenty of cover.

Alex knew that Cassie's first thought was for Majestica, the pregnant female about to give birth to the first pure mammoth. They rode toward her, and Alex prayed the beasts could tell the difference between friendly humans and deadly ones.

Abruptly, scarlet fireballs burst a hundred meters away … and another right on top of them. One of the wild grenades struck Majestica between the shoulders, and the impact knocked even the giant female battleship flat to the ground, her upper body cratered with ragged, flashburn wounds.

Cassie screamed. She threw herself off her horse and raced to the fallen pregnant female.

Alex waved his shotgun around, then took a few high potshots, hoping the retaliatory gunfire would at least stall the attackers, send them scrambling for cover. But it was a pitiful gesture at this range. None of the terrorists came out of the tree line.

Gunshots rang out and ineffectual bullets peppered the mammoth-elephant hybrids, sending them trumpeting into a frenzy. Some charged, stopped, trumpeted. But the big male Bullwinkle thundered into the night, toward the attackers hiding in the trees.

Alex dismounted and came up beside a determined but weeping Cassie. His heart wrenched, knowing they had all been betrayed. The young woman impatiently swiped tears from her eyes and got to work. "Damn, Dr. Pierce—I don't have the equipment for this!"

Back in the forest, startled shouts turned to shrieks. Alex could well imagine the giant bull trampling the bastards into paste on the ground. Bullwinkle hooted, a powerful bellow that brought more shrill screams. A grenade burst near the beast, then the big mammoth was into the trees, smashing branches, splintering trunks, following the panicked outcries.

More screams. He did not think further about what Bullwinkle was doing. He could see only the pregnant mammoth's blood shining dark and wet in the moonlight. "Don't worry. I'll help," he said to Cassie. Corporate CEO bullshit, but it seemed to be what she needed to hear. He knelt beside her, trying to anticipate what the young woman was trying to do. She worked with utter concentration, adrenaline, and desperation, staving off panic.

As he tore off his shirt and wadded it up into a large pad—nowhere near enough, he saw, pressing it into the gaping wound—he heard a faint sound and looked around. Other mammoth hybrids bellowed, but the gunfire had halted for the moment. Bullwinkle's work?

The whispery sound of feet in the sedge grasses came nearer. Cassie didn't notice it. Bare-chested, Alex backed away from the dying animal, leaving his shirt to soak up a gusher of blood. He smelled gunpowder and meat. "They're coming back," he said. Grabbing his shotgun from the trampled ground, he moved as quietly as he could around Majestica's massive bulk.

"Keep them the hell away from my mammoths," Cassie said, her voice thin. She didn't even look up from Majestica.

Alex jacked a shell into the shotgun, hoping the flat clack-click sound would be enough of a deterrent. *Never.* Halfway around the heaving beast, he crouched down, looking across the moonlit expanse.

He cursed himself as much as the fanatics. He had underestimated their dedication, dismissing them entirely. He had scoffed at their mindset, never giving them credit for a zeal that would push them beyond theoretical protests. How could they be so *vehement?* There was a long, precarious bridge between waving signs and launching missiles, but Kinsman and his Evos had crossed it.

He'd considered the Luddites to be quaint, backward, even silly. Now they had proved deadly. Causes had always attracted violent crusaders whose actions seemed inexplicably extreme to most people—pro-lifers shooting abortion doctors, environmentalists "protecting the Arizona desert" by setting fire to luxury homes. Could any ends justify such means?

The Evo crusaders came out of the trees, hunched over as they emerged from the protective shadows. They were competent enough, moving quickly, not talking. But Alex saw the reflection of their eyes as they covered the last twenty meters. Three that he could see, two headed directly this way, weapons ready … thinking they had already won.

He raised the shotgun and a lot of thoughts ran through his mind. It was easy enough to think you could shoot at an enemy, someone with a grease-blackened face and cradling a grenade launcher, pistol strapped at his waist. But when it was a kid of maybe twenty …

The kid raised an arm to his comrades, who immediately squatted and aimed—at Majestica. And Cassie!

They knew their target. They knew exactly what they intended to shoot.

And Alex had no time left for doubt. Executives, he often said to others, were people who could make decisions on time. Well, here was one. He shot the kid with a spray of pellets. He hit him in the legs, but square on.

Alex did not let himself hear the screaming as he jacked the next shell in, sighted on a man who had half-risen to his feet and was swinging a long-barreled weapon toward Alex. "Cassie, get down!" he yelled, then sighted and squeezed off the round. The feel of the gun was as natural as when he'd potted away at clay pigeons on weekends, long ago.

Now the third Evo, a woman—but she was already running away. He let the terrorist take three more strides to be sure she was out of lethal range. The blast of pellets against her shoulders and backpack did not knock her down, but she cried out, and ran even faster in a headlong stagger back toward the trees.

The first kid was yelling, rolling around with his bloody hamburger legs drawn up to his chest. The second man lay still; Alex didn't even know where he'd hit the terrorist. The woman made it to the trees, where Bullwinkle was still crashing around. Alex kept down—the Evos had plenty of distance weapons, and would be looking toward the source of his shots.

"Dr. Pierce! I need your help here!" Cassie sounded closer to panic than he had ever heard her.

Slinging the shotgun low, ready to spin around and open fire again into the night, Alex scrambled back around the dying Majestica.

✦   ✦   ✦

Helen rode hard, and her horse was hot, its mouth foaming as she careened down the bumpy jeep road. She could see the darkness of trees and night blended with probing beams of hard white surveillance lights ahead.

She and Alex had always talked about beefing up security in an apron covering the entire approach from the South Gate. When the protesters had settled in, they'd brought their own lights, as well as coolers of food and drink, so they could squat down and begin chants and drum beating in a general disruptive "people power" party. They kept it up until the early hours, youthful idealism uniting with the universal instinct to party. Annoying, certainly, and frustrating—but nothing to be taken seriously.

That had been their biggest mistake.

Occasionally, those little protests had only been a distraction, a cover for one or two Evos to slip past the fencing and guard stations in the dark. Once inside, though, they had no good idea which targets to go for, what vandalism to accomplish. Inept commandos, they generally blundered into staff housing or maintenance sheds, which had been deliberately disguised to look like laboratories and stables.

But now, the log-fronted Pleistocene Hospital was on fire. They had struck directly to the heart of the retrograde evolution project.

"Damn you," she said. "Damn you all." She kicked her horse, riding harder.

The tall pines surrounding the corral had become torches in the night, crackling resinous flames. From inside the high reinforced fences she heard a roar, an indescribable screaming cry that sounded like nothing human. Short Stuff and Middle Man, the first two mammophant hybrids, were still in there, far from the safety of the rest of their herd … brought back to the ranch buildings for regular health monitoring.

Helen dismounted from her gray mare before the horse had even come to a stop. She hit the ground running. Frightened by the noise and the smoke, the exhausted mare trotted away in confusion. The fire from the Ponderosa pines had already descended to the corral fence. She slammed through the gate, calling out to the two oldest mammophants.

Middle Man had backed to the far corner, away from the burning trees, away from the light. The big male trumpeted a sound like anguish, obviously frightened and confused. He bled from several wounds in his thick hide, but the injuries seemed relatively minor. Helen didn't even stop to consider whether Middle Man might charge her.

In the center of the trampled enclosure lay Short Stuff, collapsed to the ground like a defeated calf in a rodeo spectacle. High-powered gunshots had blasted both of her forelegs, ripping gouges in muscle and bone until the female hybrid had crashed. Short Stuff chuffed and hooted as she struggled on the grass, her legs bloody and useless appendages.

In shock, revulsion, and helplessness, Helen swayed backward, grabbed for the corral fence to support herself, but missed. Watery-kneed, she sank down, and froze, utterly unable to do anything. Short Stuff trumpeted again in unspeakable pain.

Ralph Duncan strode into the corral, swinging his head from side to side, taking in details. His eyes had always looked world-wise, as if they'd already seen everything, but now his face had a disgusted horror. "God damn! God *damn*!"

He strode forward like an avenger, holding the powerful rifle at his side. Helen made a strangled sound, and he whirled, ready to shoot, but when he recognized her, his expression instantly changed. "Miz Pierce!"

Short Stuff let out another hollow, trumpeting call. Ralph's expression hardened, and he turned away from Helen, ignoring her. Without hesitation, he marched up to the writhing, wounded mammophant, pushed the barrel of his rifle up against the base of Short Stuff's massive skull, and pulled the trigger. The hybrid groaned and slumped. Ralph shot her again, then turned back to Helen. His face was ruddy and murderous. "God damn it!"

Shaking, Helen pushed back to her feet, then grabbed the corral fence and vomited. More shouts and gunshots came from the main lab complex. Through the fence and the trees she could see flames shooting from the admin building. She coughed and spat. "How many are there? What—"

He took her arm and led her out the gate. "Middle Man's fine for now. I've got security troops split between defending the ranch and trying to fight the fires." He touched his earpiece, listened, then shouted, "Dammit, don't wait for the sheriff! Just move on it!"

Helen heard the distant patter of gunfire, military-style commands, and the frenzied shouts of shadowy attackers. They could have broken through the fences anywhere. Were these the same protesters that had innocuously waved their signs and posed for the TV cameras? Could it all have been a feint, a ploy to let Helyx security believe the Evos were ineffectual whiners and bored activists in search of a cause … when all the while they were planning this brutal strike as soon as they could get a man inside?

She saw birds fluttering in the trees, the passenger pigeons disturbed from their nests in the big oaks. "I'm going to the Hospital!" She heard sounds that could only be giant moas squawking in panic. "Ralph, get those fires put out!"

As she ran toward the Hospital, Ralph yelled louder into his voice pickup. On one side of the main admin building, a few men had set up a hose and were spraying the yellow flames on the log walls, but fiery fingers already crept along the roof.

Helen didn't give a damn about the computers and office furniture inside. She ran toward the Hospital itself where all the retrograde hybrids were kept, her life's work, the maturing ambassadors of species long extinct. Why would anybody want to harm them?

Probably the same people who break into cancer-research centers and "liberate" all the experimental animals, she thought. *I guess they don't see the contradiction.*

Out in the Hospital yard, she saw tall, ostrich-like moas set free from their cages, wandering around in terrified confusion. Brown feathers ruffled, serpentine necks swiveling about, horny beaks open with hissing squawks, they kicked up dirt with lizard-like feet and pecked at any person who came close. Ungainly dodos scrambled about like overgrown drunken chickens, honking in fright. Helen heard other animals scream and yowl from within the Hospital itself. Smoke oozed through several broken windows, growing thicker, blacker.

Just then a man with a prim face and dapper-looking clothes stepped across the porch holding a revolver in his hand. Geoffrey Kinsman. Like a grim executioner, he pointed at the dodos and methodically shot them all, moving from one to the next to the next.

Though armed with nothing but her anger, Helen raced toward him. Other protesters ran past Kinsman into the lab building, not willing to simply let the fire do its work.

Kinsman turned toward the closest frightened moa, putting three bullets through its long neck. The giant bird toppled like a fallen tree. Not even pausing to reflect on his handiwork, the man stalked toward the smashed-open door of the Hospital and vanished inside.

Helen screamed in outrage, but Kinsman didn't even notice her.

After stepping over the shattered carcasses of the magnificent lost birds, she barged into the main laboratory. Evos were overturning desks, smashing computers, dumping animal feed on the floor in a wild frenzy, like capering cannibals celebrating the arrival of a boatload of missionaries. These crusaders had no organization, no plan, just chaos.

Dressed in her jeans and camping clothes, Helen entered the lab, smelling the fire and spilled chemicals, the blood and nose-tingling gun smoke.

In the harsh, stinging smoke she saw Geoffrey Kinsman, proud slayer of helpless dodos and moas, trotting from cage to cage, shooting every creature inside. Fast, methodical, intent.

Helen's eyes burned with disgust. Ducking through the smoky light, she went to the cages on the other side, past lab furniture, desks, equipment racks. She threw open cage doors and coops, chasing the dodos, moas, and other hybrids out, giving them a chance. Squawking and hissing, the marvelous creatures ran, fleeing the fire, fleeing the gunshots.

There, dammit! The chaos grew. Shouting and gunshots echoed from outside. She heard a shrill whistle, a bull-horn. A helicopter circling.

Grinning, a blond-haired, clean-shaven man ran past her holding a long shovel, battering file cabinets, smashing beakers, computer screens, even ceramic coffee cups. He took a swipe at a waddling dodo, missed, and Helen grabbed the shovel handle, wrenching it out of his grip.

The man shrugged, then toppled a heavy laser-ROM storage rack, scattering the prismatic platters like Christmas ornaments. He snatched up a crowbar some other protester had dropped.

From nearby came the sound of a window smashing. More strangers ran in through the Hospital door, carrying weapons.

When his pistol was empty, Kinsman took a repeater assault rifle from one of the Evos, checked that it was loaded. Then he looked up and saw Helen. Recognized her.

"Damn you!" she said, raising the shovel as if it was a match for his rifle.

Behind her, the reckless blond Evo grabbed the closed doors of the larger pens at the back of the laboratory. The barricaded, reinforced rooms.

Kinsman hesitated with his rifle, smug with self-justification. "This has to be done."

With a deft twist the blond Evo pried open the lock. He must have expected nothing more than another awkward-looking bird. He held his crowbar loosely in one hand, as if ready to bash a few more animals.

And a saber-tooth cat lunged out at him, already maddened by the fire and the noise.

The big panther's front fangs gleamed, as long as scimitars. It reared up to embrace the man and with a throaty growl it bore him down, muscles moving like liquid beneath its mottled, long-furred coat. The Evo screamed as the panther/sabretooth hybrid tore open his chest, raising long curved fangs and plunging once, twice, three times.

Helen managed to shout "No!"—just as a panicked Kinsman opened fire.

✦   ✦   ✦

On the sedge grass, trampled and bloodstained, Cassie leaned over the gasping, quivering hulk of the fallen Majestica. The female almost-mammoth panted and shuddered, her body core ripped open by the grenades.

"She's dying." Cassie looked up at Alex, her eyes wide and pleading, as if somehow this important corporate executive could do something.

"Yeah," he said uselessly.

She seemed to be in a daze, saw the shotgun slung low in his hand. "You shot at the Evos?"

"Forget them."

Majestica's body heaved and clenched and trembled in spasmodic labor—dying, but also following a biological imperative. Alex heard a snorting and pounding sound and held up his shotgun, ready to defend them against a continued Evo attack—but he saw only the huge head and long curved tusks of the angry Bullwinkle. The large mammoth stomped on the ground, thrashed his shortened trunk.

In the stark, silvery moonlight Alex saw a few flecks of black blood peppering the shaggy fur, minor wounds from gunshots. He had expected to see the bull's long ivory spears coated with gore, his front feet splattered with the blood of crushed humans. But Alex heard the Evos still screaming and crashing away into the night as they fled up the valley.

The bull mammoth had let them live. Bullwinkle could easily have trampled every one into the ground. Instead, he had just driven them off and turned back to come here. At the moment, Alex himself didn't feel so civilized.

Lumbering close to Majestica, the shaggy bull sniffed, quested with his hairy trunk. Bullwinkle watched with round, wise eyes as Cassie felt the pregnant female's heaving belly, her hands exploring the quivering muscle and tough hide.

She drew her long hunting knife.

The other hybrids milled about nearby, circling and snorting, some trumpeting their pain, all clearly agitated. One of the youngest hybrids waded out to the middle of the muddy watering hole and raised its trunk high as it honked into the night.

The Evos had gone away, their destruction accomplished, leaving pain in their wake. *Making their savage point.* Alex knew he should call Ralph and his security men, bring them out here in Helyx choppers to run the terrorists into the ground, apprehend them and haul them off for Federal prosecution.

But as he knelt beside a blood-streaked Cassie, he didn't feel that was important enough right now.

The pregnant female had closed her intelligent eyes in wrinkles of dark skin, blinking only occasionally. Majestica's breath was slow and deep, a bass-noted wheezing, accompanied by a bubbly wet sound of blood and air oozing from large holes in her massive torso.

Majestica's pelt gleamed, glossy and moist. A heavy musk mixed with the metallic sourness of blood rose from the laboring mountain. The female's pelvis was tilted, her womb clenching as she used the last of her energies to squeeze.

A charge of tension permeated the air, a slow silent sense of gathering energies … of time contracting down to a completion.

Cassie pressed her hand against the distended belly. The abdominal muscles shuddered, but Majestica was clearly dying in the moonlight. Even Alex could see that. She wouldn't last long enough to give birth, and the purebred infant woolly mammoth would die inside the womb.

He knew that young Cassie had needed to sacrifice mother animals before, delivering their young by Cesarean. It was a part of ranch life when there were a lot of animals to herd and tend. In her hesitation now, he read that Cassie didn't know if her muscles and her resolve and her knife- edge would be up to the task she now faced.

Ralph's hoarse voice chirped in Alex's ear, with words so devastating that Alex could spare no attention for what the young ranch hand was about to do. "Boss, you'd better get back here." The old security chief paused, as if gathering courage. "It's Helen. Get back here now."

Cassie barely looked up as Alex ran to his horse.

Sobbing, she raised her long knife high, hesitated, then plunged it deep.

✦   ✦   ✦

When Alex rode up to the main Helyx complex, two of the ranch buildings were engulfed in flame. Fire crackled and roared, clean wood smoke mixed with the foul stench of burning electrical wires, chemicals, and plastics.

He called for Ralph, then he saw the security men dragging bodies out onto the lawn in front of the Pleistocene Hospital. His stomach lurched.

Alex had underestimated the Evos completely, the intensity of their gut-level resistance to what he was doing. And Kinsman himself, a former colleague, was someone who should have known better. Alex had rolled his eyes at the silly signs, foolishly dismissed the objections of people he considered Luddites. "It's not nice to fool with Mother Nature."

Recreating the mammoths had aroused such a passion, such a sense of wonder in his wife—but he had never considered that it might engender equal and opposite emotions in her detractors.

He called for Ralph again, but his voice broke as he stumbled across the yard. The rangy old man jogged up to him, feverish, his leathery face fallen in despair. He threw himself on Alex, both arms around his shoulders. Alex went weak with dread.

"Where is she?" he croaked, but he could tell from the stiffness in the security chief's muscles that he was already too late. "Where is she!"

Ralph staggered back. Without a word he walked with Alex toward the burning Pleistocene Hospital. In the acrid yellow glow, a few surviving animals ran about in panic. Passenger pigeons squawked from the oak trees. Others fluttered across the night sky, escaped from burning nests. Bloody mounds of feathers on the grass marked the slaughtered dodos and moas. *Extinct again.*

He took a few steps, choked on acrid smoke, turned.

Helen lay outside on the ground where Ralph had carried her. She had a crumpled, broken look, he thought abstractedly. That was when the fog began to wrap itself around him, dulling the clamor, shrouding the world in a ghostlike slowness. He shook his head, but the fog remained. His field of view telescoped away and he staggered. He reached out to steady himself on a beam and his hand felt nothing. Sour air rasped into his lungs. The iron taste of blood told him he had bitten his tongue. And the soft fingers of fog thickened.

The feathers of ancient birds fluttered around her like a halo, catching the glow of hot white security spotlights. Her flannel shirt had soaked up the crimson blood. She lay, waxen, lifeless. He did not count the gunshot wounds.

In the background he barely heard Ralph's security men shouting. Ranch workers, in shock and keeping themselves moving with forced activity, braved the inferno of the lab to rescue a few remaining experimental animals from their cages. To salvage some of the records. To preserve cellular specimens. Sometime in the distant future, he would probably thank them.

None of that mattered now.

He tried to take two steps toward Helen, but his muscles disobeyed. His knees buckled, weak and watery.

Alex collapsed, sitting on the rough ground. Close enough to see her, but she would never again be close enough to touch.

An empty man rode back out to Clement Valley. The cool night air brushed at his face, but he did not feel it. The east brimmed with a pale glow but he did not see it. The soft fog fingers were still there in his head. He shook it.

He found Cassie, her shirt and braided hair and jeans soaked with dark wetness. When he saw the blood, he had a sudden fear that she too had been shot. But she got up on unsteady legs, looking utterly exhausted in the beam of his flashlight.

Then Alex saw the small creature, like a newborn elephant but covered with matted wet fur. It stood already. About the size of a riding lawnmower. The baby mammoth moved on wobbly legs slick with its mother's fluids—aware and healthy. Somber eyes accepted him in mute communion.

Alex drew a deep breath. A mammoth, the first purebred ambassador from that extinct species, arriving on this night of smoke and blood.

He felt a trickle of amazement through his shell of despair. Though its mother had been murdered by attackers, this fourth-generation offspring had been successfully delivered alive.

In spite of all this. Thanks to Cassie.

"It's a start," she said. Her large, wonder-filled eyes stared at Alex as he touched the thick reddish fur on the young mammoth's sturdy shoulders. He knew he should tell her about Helen, but he wasn't ready to deal with the questions ... or the sympathy. He couldn't think of anything to say.

"I want to name him Adam," she continued. "Seems appropriate."

The rest of the herd huddled together in the naked night, while Bullwinkle stood near Majestica's carcass. He twitched his trunk, snorting steam plumes in the waning moonlight. Alex imagined the big bull was as anguished at losing his mate as he himself was over Helen. He heard a low, guttural note in its sighs and wheezes that had not been there before.

He turned away. Shared grief was little comfort.

The big animals clustered together, calmer now, as light seeped into the valley. Tall, powerful, magnificent. Back from extinction. Distantly, hollowly, a part of Alex thought that the throwback Evos were a portion of humanity that might be better off extinct. Not these creatures. Not these strong and wonderful miracles that his wife had brought forth from dreams.

Alex stood among the herd and looked at young Cassie, seeing her resolve undampened. She was saying something but he could not hear, somehow.

In Helen's memory, he promised himself that he would carry on this project. Even though he might have to move to the ends of the Earth, where he and the mammoths could be safe ...

Somehow.

Adam tottered off toward the herd. It waddled in the grass, lit by thin rays of sun, bleached of all color. Bullwinkle saw the small moving thing and sent a blaring trumpet salute. The herd answered with a chorus of bellows and huffs.

In this moment Alex felt his own life slip into insignificance, one more mote beneath the hard stars. One more member of a newcomer species, a mere vessel. His best work lay forever in the past now, but he could still make some difference.

The fog around him cleared, just a bit, letting in the glow of the east. Helen could live only through these creatures, through her work. He would have to speak and care and fight for his wife's memory, too, and for all of her legacy, living and dead.

Clouds were moving in, he noticed absently. It was a shrouded dawn, though it could turn bright.

Mammoth Dawn

Full Novel Treatment and Proposal

OVERVIEW

Centered around the topical resurrection of majestic woolly mammoths, sabretooth tigers, and other prehistoric creatures that became extinct during the last great Ice Age, *Mammoth Dawn* is a plausible scientific and ecological thriller only one step away from current research in genetics and paleontology. The story is filled with modern scientific techniques, a sense of wonder, and is also a relevant cautionary tale about the damage being done to the ecosystem and the diversity of life on Earth.

A passionate billionaire scientist, Dr. Alex Pierce, and the intelligent and beautiful activist, Cassie Worth, have devoted their lives to recreating the lost past and protecting the future. They collect and maintain an ambitious "Library of Earth" to store the genetic information of currently endangered species in hopes of preserving much of Nature's wealth before it becomes extinct.

As part of this work, Alex and Cassie use restored DNA taken from museums and preserved specimens to bring back wondrous extinct animals that have been eradicated through the callous mistakes of mankind—passenger pigeons, Tasmanian tigers, dodos. On a vast ranch in the wilds of Alaska, they have recreated an environment from the end of the last Ice Age, complete with dire wolves, sabretooth tigers, and a herd of woolly mammoths.

Though they are devoted to protecting the genetic diversity of Earth, Alex and Cassie must battle the human threats of radical "clean genes" terrorists, corrupt politicians, and a former Soviet power broker. They also face primal struggles against prehistoric beasts and harrowing Arctic storms. During his darkest hour, when left in disgrace by tragedies on his "Resurrection Preserve," Alex is forced to participate in the first-ever modern mammoth hunt. This challenge pits Alex's greatest enemies against each other, and against towering beasts from humanity's shadowed past.

Unlike *Jurassic Park*, the real science in *Mammoth Dawn* is *imminent*, likely to be put into use within the next decade. Cloning mammoths is not only a plausible technique, but one that has been discussed much in recent scientific journals (as described below). In addition, the message of species preservation, ecological awareness, and the need for biodiversity is relevant to all readers.

The novel is coauthored by Kevin J. Anderson, #1 internationally bestselling author with 15 million copies of his books in print in 26 languages, and Gregory

Benford, winner of the most prestigious awards in the field of science fiction, as well as respected visionary and PhD physicist. Dr. Benford proposed the "Library of Earth" project in a well-received paper published in the *Proceedings of the National Academy of Sciences.*

With a commercial concept and strong emotional resonance, *Mammoth Dawn* is a roller-coaster story that swings from high-tech suspense and scientific speculation to primal struggles for survival. Based on the most recent, and often controversial, research into mammoth behavior, as well as cutting-edge genetic breakthroughs, this story will both surprise and fascinate readers.

SCIENTIFIC BASIS—WHY MAMMOTHS? WHY NOW?

Cloning mammoths is not only a plausible idea, but one likely to be put into use within the next decade. The precise techniques have been widely discussed in the scientific journals. The most difficult technical problems have already been overcome in this stunning new way to save endangered, even extinct, animals.

Preservation teams have shown that it is possible for one species to give birth to implanted embryos from a similar species. Now visionary zoologists have combined that method with cloning to enable a cow to carry and bring to birth the rare Asian gaur, an endangered type of ox.

Several research teams are already working to implant woolly mammoth DNA into an Asian elephant embryo, the mammoth's nearest living relative. The resulting birth would be a mammoth-elephant hybrid. After several further generations crossed with mammoth DNA, the offspring would be genetically pure mammoths, brought back from extinction.

This dramatic possibility has found a fascinated audience in Richard Stone's 2001 nonfiction book, *MAMMOTH: The Resurrection of an Ice Age Giant* (Perseus). This popular book (which treats the original Benford "Library of Earth" paper in some detail) follows on two full-length specials recently aired by the Discovery Channel—both of which garnered record-breaking audiences. These programs followed several teams who track down preserved mammoth carcasses, from which they derive a great deal of biological information. Most prominently, in both two-hour specials and in Stone's book, the theme is *how to bring the mammoths back*.

The public is fascinated by the idea. Mammoths have a deep emotional resonance with human beings. Prehistoric man very probably hounded them to extinction, so resurrection of this exterminated species carries a quality of justice. Mammoths have a majesty and mystery greater than any existing species.

Further, the concept of our novel intersects and dramatizes a major public controversy. Cloning itself, in any form, generates a knee-jerk resistance in many people; however, the question posed in *Mammoth Dawn* goes even deeper. The basic technique uses *cloning* in a way that disconnects it from the human cloning controversy, yet is sure to cause fireworks.

Vehement opponents have argued against restoring any extinct species, even those that were clearly eradicated by mankind—such as the dodo and the passenger pigeon. A recent *San Francisco Chronicle* editorial condemned the idea, taking the position echoed by our novel's protesters. The concept of bringing back extinct species is a facet of biotech with real emotional resonance.

A fanciful glimpse of species resurrection has been used in *Jurassic Park* to the delight of many readers. *Mammoth Dawn* is much closer to reality and explores the issue as it will certainly occur, and *soon*—as a genuinely deep controversy, challenging our moral senses and our sense of wonder.

Prologue—The Hunt

Pleistocene Era, 10,000 B.C.—We open with an ancient mammoth hunt. A team of prehistoric hunters sets a trap, taking position in a grassy glen above a steep bluff. The hunt has already gone on for most of the day, humans showing themselves just enough that the small herd of the ever-more-skittish woolly beasts moves away toward the dead-end cliff face.

The sky is thick with clouds, the air sharp with a bite of cold. One hunter remembers stories of when the mammoths were plentiful, when the tribe had killed entire herds and gorged themselves on the meat, leaving the carcasses to be devoured by scavengers. The primitive people had built magnificent houses out of mammoth tusks and bones and covered them with hide. But times are getting harder year after year, and mammoths are becoming difficult to find. Many of the straggler beasts in the sparse forests of the tundra are sick, dying from a disease. The tribe has been able to find the bones of many mammoths, but few live creatures. Now, the hunter scouts have found one remaining herd of healthy mammoths, and it is time for a great hunt. Perhaps the last one.

As the mammoths are driven into the funnel of the trap, the hunters gather and consume a special psychotropic fern from pouches tied to their waists. This rare fern (like peyote) pumps them up, connects them spiritually with the mammoths. Humans depend on the mammoths, greatly revering them, as did Native Americans with the bison. Storytellers have painted pictures on cave walls, worshipping these woolly gods, who are so necessary for survival.

The hunters set off. The whole tribe works together, women and children banging sticks and drums. Adolescents set perimeter fires to drive the mammoths forward. Then the hunters charge in with their spears.

The mammoths stampede toward the high cliff. At the base of the bluff lie asphalt seeps, a tar pit swamp. Even if the Pleistocene hunters kill only one mammoth, they would have enough food for weeks; instead, they want to have a hunt like the old days, when the tribe could feast and celebrate the bounty of the mammoth. *[NOTE: a compelling and controversial recent theory suggests that overhunting by humans was one of the primary causes for the demise of the woolly mammoth as well as other Ice Age beasts.]*

In a terrible scene, the panicked herd rushes headlong over the cliffs. At the bluff edge, the biggest bull mammoth turns to face the hunters. One hunter, pumped up on the fern drug, faces the mammoth with his spear in a suicidal confrontation. The other hunters close in from the sides with their weapons. The bull mammoth rears, the hunters charge ... and they all go over the cliff.

Already some tribe members are scrambling down into the swamps to retrieve their prey. There will be much butchering, skinning, preserving. Amidst the carnage, broken mammoths lie in the tar pit swamp.

Some are still alive, thrashing and trumpeting their death cries. Hungry sabretooths and dire wolves stalk around the edges of the swamp, ready for the feast. Using torches, the Pleistocene tribe members try to drive them off, to defend their kill. But there is more here than the tribe could ever need.

The elders will tell the story of this day again and again, until great-grandchildren no longer believe it. Even with all the telltale signs, the cold, the disease, the dwindling herds, the Pleistocene hunters do not doubt that the magnificent mammoths will always be there.

PART I—MAMMOTH RANCH

Modern day Siberia—same location. We meet charismatic Gregor Galaev out at a paleontological site called "Mammoth Falls," where teams are excavating a huge number of preserved bones and carcasses. Before the end of the chapter, the reader will know Gregor is our villain, a cultured and suave "godfather"-style power broker who has carved out his own empire here in isolated Siberia, a former Soviet Mafia figure who has changed his name and made a new life.

Mammoth Falls is a treasure trove that makes the La Brea Tar Pits seem like an *hors d'ouvre.* The diggers have already found numerous carcasses of woolly mammoths, sabretooths, dire wolves, Pleistocene horses: an entire prehistoric environment preserved by the asphalt seep, the anoxic marsh, and the Siberian cold. Thanks to new genetic techniques, DNA from these extinct creatures is intact and extractable—enough to make the site enormously profitable.

Though he keeps a low profile, Gregor runs numerous operations—both legal and illegal—between Russia and the US, via Alaska. He is wealthy and ambitious, wanting to be respectable even in America. Gregor has entered into a partnership with a young American visionary and scientist, Alex Pierce (whom we will meet in the next chapter); Alex has amassed a fortune through his genetic patents, and has now turned his resources to studies of extinction and protecting endangered species. Alex is particularly interested in extinct animals from the Pleistocene Age, hence his connection with Gregor and the Mammoth Falls fossil site, from which Alex obtains pristine research specimens.

Running the Mammoth Falls excavation is Gregor's massive right-hand-man, nicknamed Psyk (Russian for "psycho"), a part-Eskimo, part-Siberian who spent time in Siberian gulags (and has the proud, detailed tattoos to prove it) before he fell in with Gregor Galaev. Psyk clings to a remnant of Eskimo mysticism, takes his life and his work at face value, and is totally loyal to Gregor. He looks like a thug, but is much deeper than that.

At the busy fossil dig, workers fill hoppers with cold, blackish muck, sorting brick-sized mammoth molars into bins, stacking tusks in a pile like firewood. Psyk finds a broken flint spearhead and is oddly stirred by this ancient site, as if he has been born into the wrong time and place. While Gregor is always looking to the future, Psyk is fascinated by the past.

While the two men stand at the base of the bluff, over which hunters once drove mammoth herds, Siberian workers slog around in the tar pit wearing rubber waders. They use scanners, hand-held pulse-detectors looking for anomalies in the bog.

With a flurry of excitement, the workers find a human body, naked, coated with smelly tar. They haul the corpse out of the marsh, jabbering that they may have found a perfectly preserved Pleistocene hunter. His hands are bound behind his back, his mouth gagged, his eyes still open and intact. Is it some indication of ritual sacrifice? The Moscow museum will pay handsomely for such an intact human cadaver. When they clean off the body, though, they are startled to see a modern *wristwatch* on the arm. Gregor and Psyk look at each other, sharing a smug smile.

A week earlier, one of the Mammoth Falls diggers had been caught selling fossil ivory tusks on the black market. Gregor has decided to send an appropriate warning to the other workers. He remembers standing in the moonlight watching, far enough away so the black splashes will not get on his clothes, as burly Psyk took great pleasure in drowning the man in tar.

Now the workers will talk in whispers, spreading the ominous story far and wide. And Gregor's reputation will grow.

Mammoth Ranch, Montana—Alex Pierce, the idealistic head of genetic research company Helyx, has set up an isolated ranch in Montana where he and his scientist wife Helen study extinction patterns and the loss of Nature's genetic heritage, leaving vice presidents and CEOs to handle the "drudgery of the business world." By dedicating his own resources—money acquired through successful genetic-engineering patents—Alex believes he can protect the Earth's biodiversity, with no strings attached.

He and Helen have launched a huge undertaking, compiling a "Library of Earth," a Noah's Ark that will collect and preserve genetic information of endangered species. Alex sponsors teams of "genetic bounty hunters" who collect DNA samples from around the world. [Estimates of the number of species made extinct every year vary from a few dozen to thousands; all agree that we are currently in the midst of the biggest ongoing "extinction event" in millions of years, a tragedy that is sadly unnoticed by the man on the street.]

But what good are all these genetic samples, once a species is wiped out? Alex and Helen are working on the process of "reversible extinction," by which they will bring back certain species that humans have driven to extinction, such as the dodo and passenger pigeon. They accomplish this by replacing the DNA in fertilized eggs of "close-cousin" species so that the animals give birth to hybrids which, after several generations of crossbreeding, yield a pure-blooded animal. "Extinction doesn't have to be forever!"

After the discovery of the Mammoth Falls fossil trove, Alex and Helen want to restore the magnificent menagerie that vanished in the Pleistocene Era, believed to have been hunted into extinction by humans. Alex— "Bill Gates with an even bigger social conscience"— hopes that he can reverse this terrible damage. Thanks to the wealth of viable genetic material obtained from Gregor Galaev in Siberia, Alex is well on the road to achieving his dream.

Meanwhile, Helyx Corp is in a technical race with a Japanese research team, which is also trying to resurrect a mammoth. Unfortunately, their latest generations have all spontaneously aborted. Unlike Helyx's work, the

Japanese are using a much more recent (and much less glamorous) dwarf species of mammoth, which died out only a few thousand years ago. Alex and Helen, however, are in the process of retro-breeding a full-sized *woolly mammoth*. When he announces this success, Alex will blow all of his rivals out of the water.

Helyx's work attracts a few radical protesters, "clean genes" advocates who call themselves Evos. This small but outspoken group is afraid of genetic engineering in any form, especially cloning. A handful of Evo protesters are always at the front gates of the Montana ranch, waving signs, shouting "It's not nice to fool with Mother Nature!" Convinced he is right, Alex doesn't understand this point of view and refuses to take the "Luddites" seriously.

[Because this technology is close to culmination, these arguments have already been made in the real world; for example, a recent impassioned editorial in the San Francisco Chronicle condemns the idea of restoring lost species, claiming that extinction is part of the natural process, even if such extinction was caused by man. Cloning or genetic engineering attracts violent protests; death threats have been made against the cloned sheep Dolly, and the recently announced cloned cat is under constant guard.]

Alex is interrupted by Ralph Duncan, the wiry sixty-ish man in charge of ranch security. Ralph has apprehended an Evo protester who broke through the fences and tried to make it into the back-country security zone. Alex is surprised to see that the man is a former colleague—Geoffrey Kinsman.

Kinsman worked as a lab assistant years ago when Alex and Helen did their ground-breaking research:

decompiling the mammoth genome from Siberian samples. The project yielded a remarkable set of breakthroughs, pioneering the process of reassembling fragments of fossil DNA into a complete genetic chain.

Alex and Helen properly acknowledged Kinsman's assistance, but did not include him as a coauthor on their research papers. (Being listed as a coauthor is a very important matter of prestige and survival for up-and-coming scientists.) Though he was little more than a lab assistant, Kinsman felt snubbed, and the wound festered when Alex and Helen later won the Japan Prize for their genome work, a grant of a million dollars. That money became the seed for Helyx Corp, now worth billions—and Kinsman was cut out of all of it.

Later, Kinsman professed to develop a fundamental moral disagreement over tinkering with the genomes of extinct animals—What sort of effect will these reintroduced animals have on the ecosystem? What if they carry ancient retroviruses? Are the formerly extinct creatures destined to be mere curiosities, strictly to live in museums or zoos? Helen (who is more attuned to feelings than Alex) has never entirely swallowed Kinsman's rationale; she wonders if their former assistant joined the "clean genes" Evos just because his pride was hurt.

Because of their connection, Kinsman has come to see Alex face to face, as an ambassador, hoping to "talk some sense" into him. The encounter is initially cordial; Alex jokes, "What are you doing with those clowns? You're smarter than that!" Kinsman responds, "Can't you see how restless and angry the people are? You're pushing too hard, too fast. Those Evo protesters are not crazies, just a symptom of the public's general uneasiness."

Alex tries to win Kinsman over by showing him what Helyx has accomplished. In a scene filled with wonder, Kinsman is astonished to learn that the nesting birds around the outbuildings are actually *passenger pigeons*, which have been extinct for more than a century. Inside the Pleistocene Hospital, where other animals are kept in pens and cages, Alex shows him hybrid *moas* (tall ostrich-like birds that were wiped out in the 1700s), ungainly and comical *dodos*, even a marsupial *Tasmanian tiger*. Though the work here goes against Kinsman's moral beliefs, he can't help but be impressed by the sheer technical accomplishment.

Impatient yet intrigued, Kinsman asks to see the *mammoths*. When Alex denies their existence as mere rumors, Kinsman says the big creatures have been spotted on high-resolution satellite photos. Alex can't understand how a simple protester has access to such images. What sort of friends does Kinsman have?

Still hoping to change Kinsman's mind, Alex takes him to a corral where Helen is tending two first-generation mammoth-elephant hybrids. Helen's work is actually much farther along than this, but neither she nor Alex reveals this.

Though the hairy elephants are majestic and gentle, Kinsman still disagrees with what they stand for: genetic tinkering, cloning, disrupting the natural process of extinction. When Kinsman spars with them, it is like a scientific debate between colleagues. Helen asks, "Don't you have any racial guilt? Human beings wiped these species off the face of the Earth—isn't it the right moral decision to rectify those mistakes if we can?"

Neither side convinces the other, though. Shaking his head, Kinsman leaves them with a final plea to be careful, to think about what they are doing. But Alex and Helen don't feel they have to worry about a small fringe group. After all, they are doing good work.

In Siberia, we meet young Cassie Worth—a beautiful and independent 22-year-old student and activist working for Helyx's Library of Earth project as one of the "genetic bounty hunters" trying to preserve endangered species.

She accompanies native guides in search of the rare Siberian tiger. It is high summer, the few weeks when the weather is tolerable for such an expedition, though she isn't sure the subzero cold could be worse than the hordes of gnats and biting flies that buzz around her eyes, face, ears. She can't smell anything other than the reek of potent, seemingly ineffectual, insect repellent.

Cassie's team is tired, about to give up on finding one of the rare tigers, but she exudes confidence and stamina to keep the team going. With her is Zach Browder, her lean and fiery boyfriend. Shared interests drew them together, the work saving endangered species—but their relationship is "theoretical," without any real love; Zach is too possessive, and Cassie is focused on her goal.

Stalking through the underbrush, they close on the quarry, then shoot with tranquilizer darts. The beautiful Siberian tiger falls thrashing and finally lies still. The team takes many photographs, makes measurements. Cassie collects a blood sample and peels back the animal's lips to scrape epithelial cells from the soft tissue inside the unconscious tiger's mouth. Everything is packaged in special preserving kits. "That's all we need."

Zach points out that many zoos around the world would pay a fortune for a specimen like this, but Cassie won't start down that slippery slope. He is willing to bend the rules for his own benefit, but she is not. While Helyx Corp works in Montana on perfecting the resurrection cloning process, Cassie has thrown herself into a proactive campaign, collecting vital DNA samples of species that may be gone within a few generations.

Cassie and her fellow crusaders have already collected genetic specimens from nearly a thousand important animals, many obtained from zoos but others taken directly from animals in the wild, like this rare Siberian tiger. Helyx then carefully freezes and stores the cellular samples for some later date, when cloning techniques will bring back lost animal populations.

Cassie ushers the team away before the tiger begins to stir. "Let's get out of here, so he can wake up and think we were just part of a bad dream." This wraps up their trip. Cassie and Zach prepare to get back to the main Helyx headquarters in Montana. Cassie is anxious to see how her "mother" is doing.

Alex and Helen welcome Cassie back to the Montana Ranch, after she has fought her way through the protesters. The young woman proudly delivers the Siberian tiger samples to the Library of Earth and asks about the herd. That afternoon, the three ride horses out to a distant valley in the ranch secure zone.

Cassie has grown up around animals and ranches, has the Montana version of street smarts. When they reach a dramatic overlook, Alex, Helen, and Cassie look down upon a group of woolly mammoths—magnificent beasts covered with russet fur and sporting long tusks. These are second- and third-generation hybrids, nearly purebred mammoths, closer than anything Kinsman saw. One of the females, Majestica, is pregnant and will soon give birth to the first true, genetically pure mammoth. This has been their dream for years.

Woolly mammoths went extinct between five and fourteen thousand years ago, when the glaciers retreated. Several other important species vanished at the same time as the woolly mammoths: giant sloths, Pleistocene horses, North American camels and lions, and sabretoothed cats. In addition to the stresses of extreme climate change, such extinctions were caused by skilled human hunting techniques and improved weapons, as well as new cross-species diseases and retroviruses brought by people migrating across the Bering Straits land bridge into North America.

Now, the three walk among the placid hybrids, upbeat, knowing that a real mammoth will be born soon. They camp on a hillside, relaxing, until Cassie (who is attuned to the beasts) notices that the mammoths are restless. Alex sits up in his sleeping bag, watching overhead as the fire trail from a backpack-launched rocket soars across the sky and explodes in the main ranch compound.

Through his ear implant, Alex hears Ralph Duncan shouting the alarm, rallying the security troops. Evo protesters are charging the main gate, trying to break into the compound. The administration building is also on fire. Alex transmits orders, and Helen is already running for her horse, riding to the site of the attack. Alex prays his wife will be safe under Ralph's protection.

Before he and Cassie can join her, though, gunshots crack across the pristine valley, grenade launchers, explosives. Alex wonders if the attack on the main compound is just a diversion, because the Evos have also broken in here and are trying to kill the mammoth herd. Cassie runs shouting among the animals, and Alex grabs their shotguns.

Majestica, the pregnant female, is hit by exploding rounds and suffers a mortal wound. She collapses in the meadow. The bull mammoth, leader of the herd, charges off into the forest darkness, scattering the vicious terrorists. Alex holds his shotgun ready, looking for a human target.

Cassie bends over the fallen female mammoth hybrid, but there is nothing she can do. Unless she can help the birth of the baby mammoth. She takes out her hunting knife....

Helen rides hard to the main compound, where all hell has broken loose. Inside the corral where she kept the two hybrids (the ones she showed to Kinsman), one mammophant cowers against the fence; the other moans in pain, studded with gunshot wounds and both front legs shattered from high-caliber rounds. While Helen stares in disbelief, the old ranch security chief Ralph assesses the situation and walks grimly over to the suffering hybrid. He places the rifle against its massive skull and, with one shot, puts it out of its misery.

He shouts orders to his security men, tells Helen that she must get to safety. Instead, she runs to the Pleistocene Hospital, where protesters have broken in. In horrified anger, she watches Geoffrey Kinsman stride along like an executioner with his revolver, systematically shooting all of the dodos and moas. He shows no remorse as he empties his pistol.

Helen runs into the Hospital, trying to stop the murderous protesters. The Evos continue to wreak havoc. Kinsman enters, carrying his repeater assault rifle, and recognizes his nemesis Helen; he looks startled, as if the whole thing has gotten out of hand. Alarmed, Helen runs to stop a protester at the mysterious barricaded pens in the back of the building, but he flings open the gate, pistol in hand, expecting to shoot another dodo.

Instead, a hybrid *sabretooth tiger* lunges out, maddened by the fire and smoke, and tears into the protester. Helen stands between the sabretooth and a terrified Kinsman; she raises her arms, screaming for him to stop. A panicked Kinsman, already on edge, opens fire with his repeater rifle, not even aiming....

Out in the valley, Alex and Cassie are entrenched with the mammoths, under fire from the Evos. Alex has to take potshots to keep them away. Cassie is intent on the dying female mammoth, which is heaving and shuddering. She can only hope to save the baby.

Alex receives a call from old Ralph, telling him he has to get back to the ranch compound right away. "It's ... Helen." Something in the security chief's voice makes Alex grow cold. Leaving Cassie, he leaps onto his horse and rushes back to the Pleistocene Hospital, where he finds a scene of carnage. Feathers and blood lie scattered all around, among the carcasses of the slaughtered dodos and moas. And then he spots his wife's body, lying cold on the grass with a blanket draped over her, separated from the other fallen Evo protesters....

Later, when Alex returns to the valley, at first he sees only the angry mammoths and the dead mound of Majestica. Then he notices young Cassie drenched in blood—has she been shot?!—beside a newborn mammoth baby. Cassie is fine, though, and so is the purebred mammoth. The baby stands on wobbly legs, covered with matted fur. Alive, healthy, the ambassador for an extinct species. Just the beginning.

Alex has developed this project because of Helen's dream, and he promises to keep it alive. Thanks to their work, a genuine mammoth has finally been born—the first in more than five thousand years—and Alex will nurture that dream, in Helen's honor. He will find a place where he can continue his work.

Part II—The Resurrection Preserve

Five years later. High in the cloud forests of Ecuador, Cassie Worth climbs a rugged slope to where she has learned a giant Andean condor is nesting. Only 80 of the huge birds survive; zoo specimens have died, and the species looks doomed. Zach Browder climbs with her, anxious to be with Cassie. As they climb, she thinks of Sinbad stories and his adventures with the giant Roc. Reaching the nest, like a fortress made of branches, they find the mother condor gone, the eggshell smashed, and a recently dead fledgling. Grim, Cassie takes her samples, confident that the genetic material will help the species to live again.

As they descend, it becomes apparent that there is friction between Cassie and Zach. He's ready to pack up their camp and head down into the Amazon rainforests in eastern Ecuador, but Cassie is ready to go home. They have been out in the wilds for much of the past several years, running from specimen to specimen. She and Zach have been lovers, bound by a common goal but without getting emotionally closer. Cassie feels that she should go help Alex Pierce with the *real* work, back in his huge new preserve in Alaska....

After the Montana disaster, Cassie went off on her own, securing a few university grants and stipends from private foundations, but she and her crusaders rapidly stalled for lack of funding. She remembers sitting with Zach in the middle of a very small, very empty apartment decorated in orange crates, cinderblocks and plywood. They are both dejected; the money has run out, and unless they find a sponsor, all their work will be for nothing. Checkbooks clamp tight as soon as the philanthropists smell a note of desperation in a cause. "Looks like we're as extinct as the animals we're trying to save," says Zach.

Unexpectedly Alex Pierce appears at her apartment door. He looks much harder, older—but still the man Cassie remembers. "I can't let all of Helen's work just die because of my grief. I need you back, both of you. We have to continue the Library of Earth project. It's got to be done."

He has purchased a giant chunk of Alaskan wilderness and entered into a business partnership with Gregor Galaev to create a "Resurrection Preserve," far from protesters and prying eyes. Galaev has also purchased an estate of his own (Zach thinks the two men are fashioning themselves as feudal lords in Alaska).

Cassie sees that Alex is no longer so cocky and aloof, no longer laughing at stupidity in the world. Before, he and his wife had paid far too little heed to the violence inherent in the Evo cause; they underestimated the lengths to which the protesters would go. Full of hubris, they did whatever they wanted to do, ignoring the warnings of others. But Alex will never make such a mistake again.

So Cassie agrees, knowing that Helyx Corp can fund all of the expeditions she had hoped for—like this one in Ecuador. Zach comes along so he can be with her, but he is immature, considering it an adventure or a game.

After bagging the Andean condor specimen, Cassie says she is tired of running from her true obligations. Their relationship has cooled, and Zach had hoped that the Ecuador trip would rekindle Cassie's feelings for him, but the opposite has happened. She tells him they are through, that she is accepting a position in Alaska to help Alex with the work in the Preserve. Zach has always known Cassie's unspoken attraction for Alex and is jealous. Rather than leaving her for good, though, Zach also accepts a job at the Preserve, where he can still be close to her. He also has ideas of how he can work the system....

Alex, haunted by the setbacks he has suffered, stands in an observation room in the Alaskan Preserve. Pickup surveillance screens track the animals around the sonic fence line. On one screen, a herd of mammoths munches on marshy growth; on another, a full-grown sabretooth cat sprawls in the sun on a flat rock. Alex has been called a modern-day Noah, but he isn't doing his work to impress anybody, just to honor Helen's memory.

His business partner Gregor Galaev has helped him to create this wondrous place. The only apparent failure so far has been the reintroduction of dire wolves: Once a most successful species, packs of ferocious dire wolves have not fared well in Alaska. Physically stronger and with more powerful teeth and jaws than modern wolves, dire wolves could bring down large animals such as bison and North American camels. Alex has already ushered the hybrids through several generations until he turned the dire wolves loose within the Preserve wilderness. Most of them apparently died, though. For some species, he decides, extinction is not reversible after all.

Alex can't allow himself any doubts about the resurrection project, because that would mean Helen may have died for nothing. In his heart, though, he realizes that if they had just moved a little slower, been more attentive to the raw nerves they were jabbing, then the tragedy might not have happened.

At first, Alex had tried to bring the Evos to justice, but though many were arrested and convicted, Kinsman—the obvious ringleader—managed to walk. Witnesses disappeared, evidence went missing, convenient "technicalities" were found during trials. Incomprehensibly to Alex, media coverage was *sympathetic* to the protesters; there seems to be a deep, ingrained resistance to bringing back extinct animals. But Alex still passionately believes he is doing a *good* thing.

Kinsman himself continues to cause trouble by rallying like-minded Luddites in Washington, DC. Hearings are coming up. Kinsman will push the Evo cause. Alex plans to be there, too, unannounced—he wants to state his own case, and look Kinsman in the eye as he does it.

Geoffrey Kinsman is dressed as an American tourist in Japan, waiting in line to see the successful and popular dwarf mammoth project. The Japanese team (Alex's rivals in Part I) has achieved their goal of bringing back the extinct species of "mini-mammoths" that died out only a few thousands of years ago.

As Kinsman stands among the excited members of the crowd, he intensely searches for any evidence of diseases. Angry, he sees a definite threat here. He is still scarred and hardened from the deadly Evo raid on the Montana Ranch, but what had appeared to be a total victory now seems to amount to nothing. Alex Pierce continues his research, only farther away in the Alaskan wilderness. But at least Alex keeps his work in extreme isolation—this Japanese team, on the other hand, treats their mammoth abominations like circus elephants, providing them to zoos around the world, letting the public get very close. Too close.

He is concerned that these animals have been restored complete with the genetic flaws or retroviruses that led to their extinctions in the first place. In addition, Kinsman resents the very concept that someone would go to all the work to resurrect an extinct species, just to keep them in zoos. The dwarf mammoth he sees does not look particularly healthy, and the Japanese are very cagy about revealing their survival and success rates. He wants to discover the truth, but has no way of compelling the Japanese researchers to share their statistics. If he had the right evidence or samples, he has powerful, like-minded friends who could see that the Resurrection Preserve is shut down in Alaska.

Kinsman is driven to find proof that he has been correct in his objections all along, and that means more than just scientific acceptability. If he can show that he was right all along, then he can justify his unintentional killing of Helen Pierce when the Montana assault got out of hand. He tries to gather incontrovertible proof that the formerly extinct mammoths do indeed pose a threat to humanity. Then he might be viewed as a savior, not a paranoid crackpot. He thinks of how many terrible retroviruses could be lurking in prehistoric DNA, plagues extinct for thousands of years, and now brought back through the meddling of man.

Kinsman is horrified to see children riding on the backs of mini-mammoths in a carnival at the Tokyo zoo. What if there is a disease endangering anyone exposed to it? He can't wait to face the Senate committee, which is a perfect platform to raise the fears of the public.

An unmarked cargo plane lands at night on an isolated airstrip in distant Samarkand. The plane is met by the vehicles, guards, and escorts of a powerful clan leader, Uruk Bey. Bey is dressed in colorful garb, heavy jewels, dueling daggers as well as a small pistol. His black eyes, though, seem the most dangerous part of him.

The aircraft hatch opens and Gregor Galaev emerges, impeccably dressed, looking completely fresh even after the long flight. Gregor greets the rugged clan leader as they walk around the cargo plane. Bey looks very eager, his black eyes hungry. Gregor and Bey are both avid big-game hunters and they have bagged several prize specimens together.

Inside the cargo hold, Gregor unveils a large reinforced cage that contains a breeding pair of dire wolves, powerful and muscular wolf-precursors from the Pleistocene Era. The black-furred predators look fierce, stockier than modern wolves, with golden eyes. They snarl and try to bite the cages; the bars already show silvery marks where their fangs have worked on the metal during the long flight. Uruk Bey is impressed. He laughs heartily. The dire wolves will be wonderful guardians, running wild around his walled citadel. In a few years, after several litters, he might even have enough to choose one for a very special hunt. Uruk Bey looks as wolfish as the predators in the cage.

Gregor has smuggled the beasts out of the Resurrection Preserve. He has tightened his ties with the loner Alex in a mutually beneficial relationship. Many of the artificially bred dire wolves have died out in the wild, and the species has not been as fecund as expected in their new environment. Even Alex, with his careful tallies of species and reintroduction patterns, won't notice these two missing. Gregor feels no compunction against slipping a few of the animals out for discerning collectors and fellow hunters, such as Uruk Bey. After all, the Preserve is Gregor's investment, too.

Uruk Bey takes his dire wolves, motioning for his guards to drive a flatbed cargo truck up to the plane, surrounded by military jeeps. Gregor stands by, watching as handlers drive the old truck, which toils along an unpaved road into the Samarkand hills, where the clan leader lives in his citadel. The black-market money Gregor just received for these two animals alone would have bought him an entire city in the old Soviet Union....

After returning from Ecuador with the condor sample, Cassie and Zach get to work on the preserve. Alex congratulates both of them on a job well done. Cassie is obviously attracted to him, and Zach is sour, knowing she has slipped through his fingers, but they are not young Turk students any more. He wants to keep world hopping, happy-go-lucky and feeling superior because he is doing Meaningful Work. To him, the Library of Earth project is a feather in his cap, a trophy, but it is truly the dream that drives Cassie's life.

No longer just a spunky ranch hand with an intuitive feel for animals, she is now an expert in her field. Cassie is in charge of the Library of Earth database, a high-tech storage area for genetic samples. Already, viable cells have been preserved from thousands of endangered species, but even with all the resources of Helyx, they can never keep pace with the rate at which humans are wiping out species worldwide. "So many extinctions every year!"

Alex is called to Washington, DC to defend his work, though after the Montana debacle and the obviously corrupt investigation of the Evos, he doesn't trust the altruism of the government. Alex meets with his lawyer Randall Levay, planning their strategy. The two walk through the DC zoo, talking about the impending hearings. Their conversation takes place in front of a new exhibit full of giant pandas, which had once been on the verge of extinction. Thanks to cloning technology similar to what the Helyx Corp is using, the slow-to-reproduce pandas have been brought back to viable numbers again. Helen would have been so pleased to see this....

Kinsman, dressed in fine clothes and looking professional and businesslike, gives his testimony to a Senate committee investigating genetic research. He is confident in his speech, very reasonable; he has given such "sermons" many times before. He speaks to a panel chaired by Sylvia Chesney, an ambitious, attractive Senator from Alaska. Kinsman talks about the dangers of unknown retroviruses "hidden by the labors of time" being reintroduced to the environment, "thanks to the bull-in-a-china-shop work of Helyx and others."

He makes a passionate case that numerous diseases could be buried within the DNA of certain species, retroviruses to which no human being has any immunity. "By squeezing mammoths out of a test tube, Helyx Corp will also bring back everything else buried in their very genes, horrible diseases that could well jump species, just like AIDS jumped from monkeys to humans, like Ebola came out of a cave in Africa. Can we afford to take that risk?"

Helyx's crack lawyer Randall LeVay vehemently objects to this alarmist scenario, pointing out that "Mr. Clean Genes" has no basis whatsoever for his paranoid imaginings. Despite Kinsman's repeated investigations and studies, he has yet to find any evidence of unusual diseases.

Then, like Bill Gates testifying at the Microsoft trial, Alex arrives unannounced to a media-circus in front of Senator Chesney's committee. Nobody is more surprised to see him there in person than the Senator herself. Glaring daggers at Kinsman, he responds to the supposed dangers of "rescuing innocent species from the abyss of extinction. Human greed and short-sightedness have wiped numerous species from the face of the Earth. Now, human ingenuity can rectify those wrongs."

Alex is a charismatic defender. He brings his own genetic samples taken from woolly mammoths at his Resurrection Preserve and insists they're clean. Cassie Worth has run extensive analyses of his mammoths and has found no evidence of any retrovirus.

Next, Senator Karl Fitch makes a passionate speech in favor of the Evos, and of caution. Alex suspects that Fitch, who has always argued against Helyx's work, may be the high government figure supporting his enemy Kinsman—because plainly, somebody powerful is. Fitch rants, but fumbles to a halt every time Alex presses him for hard data to support his grand pronouncements. Most of the spectators see him as a spiteful bag of wind.

As the highly emotional hearing winds down, Senator Chesney sides with the Resurrection Preserve—it is, after all, an engine that drives part of her state's economy, just like the oil pipeline—and she chews Kinsman out for shoddy science. "This Committee must base its conclusions on *facts* rather than fantasies, however plausible you may consider them to be." The Committee itself is about to enter a two-month recess, and the Senator is returning to Alaska.

In a sudden transition, we next see Senator Chesney sweating, laughing, making love—with Gregor Galaev.

They are in his big estate house. This is clearly not the first time they have been lovers.

Though he at first planned this to be an affair of convenience, Gregor has become involved with the Senator. Sylvia Chesney was married to a millionaire who supported her run for the Senate. He died shortly into her first term, and now she knows that in a year she will face a tough reelection. In Washington she has gotten caught up in the thrill of power. She wants more, but she is from a minor state. "Alaska is so huge yet insignificant at the same time!" She sees Gregor as a way to help her ambitions; for him, Sylvia is the essence of America.

The Senator is cagey. She has to be careful with her public responses to the controversial Resurrection Preserve, of which Gregor is a major partner. She dons a fine Chinese robe and joins Gregor and his charming teenage daughter Raisa for a nice lunch. Raisa knows about her father's affair and doesn't mind at all; she and Sylvia get along like good friends, unlike Raisa's relationship with her real mother back in distant "civilized" Moscow.

We also meet the henchman Psyk's teenage son Nikolai (whom Psyk has taken from his mother in the US). Nikolai is a young copy of Gregor's lieutenant, very much in awe of his father; he is quite devoted to young Raisa, like a bodyguard. (He adores her, but like a medieval knight devoted to the queen, not in a realistic romantic sense.) Inside Gregor's house are numerous stuffed animals, hunting trophies from his expeditions—including a beautifully mounted (and highly illegal) Siberian tiger, the same endangered species Cassie was trying to rescue in a previous chapter....

Later that day, on an outing, when the Senator is ready to return to Juneau, Gregor's security screen picks up two curious telejournalists who are trying to expose the Senator's liaison. She is furious at how much incriminating evidence they have captured with their high-tech microcameras. Gregor is just as upset; he has much to hide, many crimes in his past, many prices on his head.

He uses the old Siberian solution, arranging for the telejournalists to end up in a "new gulag" mining camp across the Bering Straits, for good. Sylvia is mesmerized by his casual use of power, which to her has a sexual edge. She knows about his former identity in the Soviet Mafia, but even though there are international warrants out for his arrest, Sylvia thinks she can take advantage of his connections and power base. The Senator secretly believes she has a chance to be chosen as the state's next governor, if she finds her own "big issue" that a lot of people can get behind. Gregor has a way to give her that Big Issue.

After the Senator rejoins her staff back at the capital, Gregor goes into his private sitting room with a roaring fireplace, stuffed bears and lions, carved elephant tusks, the horn of a rare white rhinoceros. He takes a seat next to one of his ferocious-looking trophies, leans back, and closes his eyes—but not to relax. He is preparing himself to "hold court." He has not hurried himself with Sylvia, but he knows other people are waiting for him, important men who are owed favors … or who owe him favors.

The first man to come in looks rail-thin and weak, gray-skinned, on death's doorway. Gregor is shocked to see how much the man has changed. This is Commissar Stepan Orkov, Gregor's former Soviet boss, who has fallen into political obscurity and become the mayor of a polluted Siberian town. The Commissar is riddled with cancer. Gregor makes no comment on the man's appearance, pours them both a snifter of expensive Georgian brandy (though Orkov only looks longingly at his and does not take a drink).

He explains to Gregor about his hellish, ineffective cancer treatments. He is dying. He begs Gregor for help. This is a telling scene, demonstrating that Gregor Galaev is so powerful in his own microcosm that people believe he has the power of life and death.

Gregor (which is not his real name) came across to the US from Siberia as a "worker" in the usual crime industries—trading everything from assault carbines, drugs and medicines, machine guns, and the ever-popular Kalashnikov, on up to helicopters, anti-aircraft missiles, submarines, enriched uranium, and plutonium.

More intelligent and more ambitious than his comrades, he understood the demands of the trade. He once forced a woman to eat gravel, to show respect, after she had stolen tip money from the strippers in a club. He learned how to stash gold and diamonds in bootheels or in hollows specially worked into pianos and chairs. Slowly and quietly, "Gregor Galaev" made a name for himself.

Now, he explains that he can do nothing to cure the old commissar's cancer, but Orkov only asks if he can ease his pain, make his miserable life tolerable. He has tried the regular painkillers, even illegal drugs, but they are either too weak or make him feel even sicker.

Gracious and smiling, Gregor brings out a container of moist chopped plant material, dense and aromatic, like a kind of hashish. "Let me give you something very rare, old friend. Potent and remarkable. It will let you go calmly to the end." It is a legendary shamanistic drug made from a nearly extinct fern that still grows around isolated high Siberian villages. These ferns are greatly sought after by native Yakuts for hallucinogenic cultural ceremonies.

Thanks to the Resurrection Preserve, these ancient bog ferns are now thriving, due in part to a symbiosis with mammoth dung, an ingredient that has been missing from the landscape for nearly ten thousand years. Gregor hopes there will soon be a burgeoning supply for the black market. While Alex Pierce dabbles with his high-minded ideals, Gregor intends to make a lot of money from the Preserve.

Grateful, the old Soviet boss departs with the narcotic fern. Gregor has just enough time to compose himself again and sip his expensive brandy before a smartly dressed Chinese businessman—Hector Chu—is ushered into the fire lit trophy room. From his expression and demeanor, Gregor can tell immediately that the businessman is going to request something very difficult.

But Gregor will manage it, as always.

Returning from Washington, DC, Alex has a regular business meeting with his investor and partner, Gregor Galaev. Both men are powerful and rich, but come from utterly different cultures. Instead of sitting in a boardroom and talking like businessmen, they ride horses to one of the lakes in the great preserve. Alex raises an automated bridge that makes a path across the water, and they cross to the island habitat where the dodos and moas live.

Theirs is a complex relationship, based at first on a simple trade of favors. Each holds a different type of power, and a hidden admiration for the other's kind. Alex knows that Gregor works both sides of the law and both sides of the Bering Straits, but since Alex has had his own extreme disappointments with US government and law, he does not pass judgment on the Siberian.

The two men met over twenty years ago, when Gregor Galaev was selling bits of frozen mammoth and sabretooth tissue that Helen and Alex first analyzed (in their famous genome-sequencing paper that neglected to include Geoffrey Kinsman as a coauthor). Since then, they have forged a good working relationship. Politically savvy and happy to do deals behind closed doors, Gregor knows how to smooth ruffled feathers. Hard-driven Alex is focused on his grand goal and not concerned about stepping on toes. He doesn't care about the Luddite Evos, but Gregor understands "the power of ignorance."

As they look at the exotic once-extinct birds, Gregor subtly reminds Alex of all the favors he's done for the Resurrection Preserve. Unfortunately, Gregor makes calm assumptions that a person should repay one favor with another, while Alex is much more of a "face value" sort of man and expects his peers to talk straight with him.

Then Gregor drops his bombshell: He would like to kill one of the mammoths in the herd so that he can obtain a pristine set of fresh *mammoth tusks*. It is simply a business proposition, for which they will be well paid. Gregor has all the details worked out. Perhaps they need to thin the herd, or a specimen for dissection and study? Gregor can think of many customers who would pay a premium for a sample of mammoth steaks, too—a caveman banquet!

Alex is offended, appalled, and turns him down flat. "What on Earth could you want the tusks for?" Gregor is surprised that Alex doesn't have some inkling about how valuable such things are in the black market.

"It was a request someone made of me." A request Gregor cannot deny, and it would be in terribly bad taste for Alex to ask about details. They are business partners, and Gregor has never denied Alex any reasonable request.

Upset, Alex says he could never shoot down one of his prize beasts just so some collector can have a trophy! It goes against the principles of the Preserve. Gregor is just as annoyed. Does this hugely wealthy man know nothing of how power is used? Incredible! "Now that we have brought back these creatures, why can we not benefit from them? You have a herd of a hundred mammoths—why is it wrong to profit from one?" It is idealism versus commercialism, and Alex doesn't realize what an affront he has just given Gregor.

Alex, after having defended his work to the Senate Committee, after facing down a nutcase like Kinsman, now can't believe that his own business partner wants to start killing off their Pleistocene specimens. He says absolutely not, in a tone that allows no argument … but Alex doesn't even realize that it is Gregor who runs the Preserve behind the scenes, while he buries himself in his Library of Earth work. And Gregor Galaev is not a man who takes *No* for an answer.

✦   ✦   ✦

Inside the fabulous Main House, Cassie studies detailed projection maps of the Resurrection Preserve, ecosystems in progress. She is working on adding minor bits of the ecosystem: extinct plants, fungi, ferns, birds. Alex calls it "background detail," the brushstrokes that paint an ancient landscape.

Cassie avoids personal problems by submerging herself in work, as if hoping to impress Alex with her abilities. In her heart, she has loved him for a long time, but Alex is too wrapped up in his mission. He hasn't even bothered to notice her as a woman, probably still remembers her as the spunky ranch hand.

She wanders among the various plants in the greenhouse, new flowers, herbs, and weeds under development from La Brea and Mammoth Falls samples. There is a new worry: allergies and hay fevers have sprung up in and around the preserve. Workers and visitors to the Resurrection Preserve often suffer from new allergies, sniffles, and sinus infections. Alex once jokingly called it the "Pleistocene flu," hay fever from the last Ice Age. But Geoffrey Kinsman and his Evos had vehemently cited this as proof that people are already vulnerable to resurrected plants and their toxins.

Cassie is interrupted by Zach Browder, ostensibly for business reasons to discuss the scheduling and staffing of several new Helyx-sponsored Library of Earth specimen-gathering missions. Cassie has compiled databases of desired samples, sending requests to zoos around the world that have rare animals in captivity. Saving the world is a full-time job.

But there is also romantic tension in the air. As far as Cassie is concerned, their relationship is over, but Zach doesn't want to let it go.

✦   ✦   ✦

Now that Kinsman has spoken to the Senate Committee—a showcase speech, from which he expected to make no tangible progress—he understands that he must take his Evos into a new phase of active sabotage again.

He has *had it* with politicians and lawyers, though some of them do see his side of things. It was no accident that he was never charged with the murder of Helen Pierce at the Montana Ranch. Kinsman has tried to go through regular channels, but in his mind the government wants to hold meetings to discuss the dangers of fire, while the resurrection work is already a blaze out of control. Luckily, many of the Evos feel the same way. The front is *here*, in the corrupted Alaskan wild, the only place where they can make the necessary impact.

A low-flying unmarked plane drops Kinsman and his team into the wilds, decked with new outdoor gear and wilderness survival supplies (surprisingly modern military gear, more than any group of protesters should be able to afford). Kinsman follows a tracker signal and discovers a mysterious stash of air-dropped crates in the dense forests outside the Resurrection Preserve.

Kinsman is accustomed to roughing it, to slipping through the wilderness, leaving no trail. Opening the crates, the Evos find sophisticated and expensive state-of-the-art weapons, along with plenty of ammunition. The reader will suspect that this equipment is far better than anything this small fringe group should have; much of it is not even on the market (black market or otherwise).

Kinsman distributes the stash of weapons to his teammates. "We can be a thorn in Alex Pierce's side … and then a stake through his heart."

Zach Browder runs the perimeter fence line of the Preserve, upset with Cassie's growing coldness and subconsciously resenting Alex. As he has done many times before, Zach easily finds ways to justify his actions.

His job is to keep watch, to make immediate repairs, to check the security zones. He flies in a small "chopter," a lightweight 2-person helicopter, on his patrol. Setting down near one of the fence substations, he goes out to tinker with the generators, and it soon becomes apparent that he is subtly sabotaging it; he sets a specific delay to bring down a certain section of the sonic fence for a limited time. He changes the frequency on his radio and transmits a brief OK signal. "Mr. Galaev, your people will have an hour before the fence goes back up. Don't be late." "Acknowledged."

He has been involved in some of Gregor's poaching and black-market activities and knows Cassie would hate him if she ever found out. But since she has cooled toward him and broken off their relationship, he has rationalized more and more. After all, he sees no harm in what he's doing. He remembers when their team was scraping out a few dollars at a time and begging civic clubs for donations. Pure idealism never got him anywhere. Yes, this is better.

He flies away in his chopter and in a clearing in the dense forest he looks down to see a large bloody carcass and the signs of a battle in the snow. Warily setting the chopter down, he climbs out to see a dead Kodiak bear—more massive than the largest grizzly—torn to pieces. Zach can't imagine what could possibly have done this to such a monster.

Around him is eerie silence. As he stands near the dark shelter of thick pine trees, he feels his skin crawl, as if something is watching him. He tenses up and begins edging back toward his chopter. Zach feels he's being watched. He hears rustling sounds in the trees, and low, synchronized growls. Not taking any chances, he races back to his chopter and takes off.

✦ ✦ ✦

With a part of the Preserve's high-tech fences bypassed, Gregor's burly right-hand-man Psyk leads a group of men on snowmobiles inside. They have high-powered guns, even a grenade launcher—everything they will need to kill a woolly mammoth. Psyk does not question his boss's orders.

Psyk's personal law is the "old way," not US or Russian law. He wants to raise his son Nikolai in the old traditions, to keep him tough and strong. Years ago Psyk had married an American woman, the boy's mother, but he hated the soft, civilized way his wife was bringing up the boy—TV, Internet, CDs, videogames, all of Western culture. Psyk had beaten her in frustration, as many Russian men did with their wives, but rather than learning her lesson, the bitch had pressed charges. In the Soviet Union, beating a woman was never much of a crime; in the US, though, it was called domestic violence. Psyk found himself in an American jail for six months.

When he was released, he contacted Gregor Galaev to make arrangements, then kidnapped his son (who was then 11) and told his wife, with utter conviction, that he would kill her himself if she tried to track them down. Then he and Nikolai moved to Alaska to work for Gregor. He has never heard another word from his wife since.

Despite his violent nature, Psyk really loves his son, and Nikolai feels the same toward his father. Nikolai is a "chip off the old block." As he and his comrades race across the snow, looking for the mammoth herd, Psyk wishes his son could have come along on this mammoth kill.

The team finds a monstrous bull mammoth, a giant creature with long curving tusks, a thick coat, and long trunk. Psyk stops the snowmobiles at a distance, and then goes by himself to approach the mammoth. Amazed, he walks forward like Crocodile Dundee in a mesmerizing trance. In a spiritual experience, Psyk comes closer and closer, eyes locked with the mammoth's. They seem to be connected across the gulf of time. Human hunters, not so different from Psyk, long-ago followed the mammoths across the tundra, surviving in the shadow of advancing glaciers, a life-and-death relationship as tight as that of the plains Indians and the bison herds. As Psyk approaches, the bull mammoth raises its prehensile trunk.

An explosion rings out. A great chunk of meat splatters from the hump on the mammoth's shoulders. Psyk stumbles backward, and Gregor's other henchmen open fire again, shooting the mammoth's legs out from under it, a very messy and painful job, though none of the wounds is immediately fatal. The mammoth thrashes and writhes on the ground, bloodying the snow, as the hunters rush forward on their snowmobiles.

Psyk is appalled at the bad kill and yells at the others. "I had him! He was mine!" One of the men—Yuri—claims that he got nervous watching Psyk so close to the monster. A third henchman comes forward with a buzzing chainsaw and bends over the tusks of the still-quivering mammoth.

After hearing the report of the torn-apart Kodiak bear, Alex and Zach fly the chopter out to inspect the carcass. Zach is uncomfortable with Alex, resenting that the head of Helyx always gets whatever he wants; the real root of his resentment comes from Cassie's obvious attraction to Alex, but Zach convinces himself of less emotional motivations.

Alex peers out the chopter windows as they cruise low over the ground—but he sees a bigger disturbance in the distance, something brown and red against the snow. The bear is forgotten as they look down in horror at the fallen butchered mammoth. Big birds, Pleistocene condors, take flight as the modified scout helicopter comes in for a landing. Alex goes white as he recognizes the carcass, mangled and bloody, its tusks hacked off.

Appalled, the two men get out of the puttering chopter and go to the giant corpse. This was not done by any predator, but by poachers. Zach is sickened. "A damn dirty kill." The beast was brought down with exploding bullets. Its tusks were probably hacked off while the creature was still alive. Remembering Gregor's "request," Alex has no doubt who is responsible for this massacre.

Though it is by now late afternoon, he instructs Zach to fly them over to the main mammoth herd and the food depots so he can verify that the rest of the great animals are safe.

Geoffrey Kinsman and his group of Evo saboteurs use special scrambling devices to bypass the Preserve's barricade fences and motion sensors. They wear slick camouflage suits and enter the isolated boundaries of the Resurrection Preserve on sleek, silent snow-skimmers, a fancy cross between snowmobiles and hovercraft.

He has been sent in here for the sole purpose of being a fly in the ointment, a wrench in the works. He will gain from this what he calls *cultural momentum*—to make the world listen to the broad, anti-biotech agenda he has made his life's work. Though part of him still admires the amazing technical achievement Alex has created, in a scientific sense, Kinsman strikes the mammoth "monstrosities" in the same way John Brown gave himself to the struggle against slavery.…

Together, the group of saboteurs race toward a large, open storage shed in a mammoth and caribou grazing area, which was pinpointed by sophisticated satellite imagery. These storage sheds are placed in strategic spots to enrich the diet of the mammoths. Kinsman and his crew douse some of these depots with fuel and set them alight, creating giant bonfires to destroy the feed supplies.

Meanwhile, on their way from the mammoth carcass, Alex and Zach observe the fire at the feed depot. As they race in, they also spot the Evo vandals running from the light of the rising arson fires. Alex descends, shouting through the aircraft's loudspeakers. The Evo snow-skimmers race into the forests for protection. Kinsman and his crew split up, knowing their rendezvous. In the gathering darkness, Alex and Zach pursue the saboteurs in the chopter. Alex is angry and baffled—is Gregor somehow in league with Kinsman's Evo fanatics? It doesn't seem possible!

When Alex cruises close to his quarry, though, Kinsman removes an EMP pulser (a high-tech weapon that a simple protester shouldn't have) and uses it to shut down Alex's chopter, frying all his electrical systems. Zach has been flying low and manages to land with a crunch in a snowdrift, shaken but unharmed. The Evos get away.

In a warehouse on his own estate, Gregor meets with the dapper Chinese businessman, Hector Chu. This time, though, Gregor doesn't have the patience for amenities. He has Psyk pry open a large crate that contains the curved tusks of the slain mammoth—the only fresh, intact ones in the world for 10,000 years. Blood still cakes the raw ends.

This man has helped Gregor run pleasure ladies across the Amur River, from China into Russia, as well as smuggle black-market materials in the other direction. He has owed the Chinese businessman a favor for a long time. "My personal cost in obtaining these tusks was much higher than I had anticipated." He may have caused an irreparable breach between himself and Alex. "I trust you will consider that any and all debts I owed to you are now paid in full?"

"Without question," the Chinese businessman says, stroking the smooth ivory surface of the tusks.

Taking his beloved son Nikolai, Psyk goes into the forest and brings with him a large dose of the psychotropic fern.

Since the terrible slaughter of the mammoth for its tusks, Psyk has felt dirty and disturbed. It goes against his grain to kill such a magnificent beast just so a three-piece-suit businessman can make an unearned trophy of its tusks. The kill was *not honorable*.

He remembers an old Yakut hunting chant about how great hunters long ago had taken a shaman drug before they went out to find their mammoth. This is an ancient oral tale, never written down, never revealed to anthropologists. He tells it to Nikolai, bonding more closely with his son. Psyk then takes the fern drug in the cold forest under dark and cloudy skies, and has his own vision. In the eerie dream sequence, he confronts a spirit mammoth, sees how the old hunts used to take place, and knows that this is how the relationship between humans and the giant beasts should be. The ancient fern, resurrected by modern technology, has unlocked these truths for him.

Next day, an infuriated Alex goes to Gregor's nearby estate. He barges in, surprising Gregor at lunch with his daughter Raisa, accompanied by Psyk's tough son Nikolai. Nikolai is like a carbon-copy of his burly father, and he guards Raisa the way Psyk guards Gregor.

Alex accuses him of killing the mammoth and of being in league with the Evos. Gregor denies any knowledge of Kinsman's activities, though he avoids answering about the mammoth. He is annoyed at Alex's bluntness; this isn't the way business is done. "I have as much right to the resources of the Resurrection Preserve as you do. You alone do not own all the rare animals."

"I don't *own* any of them—I didn't breed them to be pets or trophies or zoo specimens!"

Gregor frowns at Alex's naiveté. "You may be a scientific genius, Dr. Pierce, but you do not understand some very simple things." In truth, Gregor doesn't really need Alex anymore; he has been shipping embryos and samples to a preserve of his own in Siberia. Very soon, he will have everything he needs in a wilderness completely unregulated by silly environmental protection laws.

Psyk's son looks ready to take Alex apart, piece by piece, as soon as Gregor gives him a nod. But suave Gregor tries to defuse the situation. He has lost all respect for Alex. "You have insulted me, but even that is in my power to forgive. However, you have upset my daughter, and that is much more difficult to ignore. Go back and hide behind your fences, and hope you lose nothing more valuable than a single mammoth."

Humiliated and disturbed by Gregor—who seemed a complete stranger, treating Alex as if he were nothing more than an underling, an insect—Alex is also enraged by the Evos, remembering what they've done in Montana. He knows Gregor has a lot of strings to pull, but he fears the Evos might cause more immediate damage. They pretend to be "reformed" but Alex doesn't buy it.

Alex returns to his Pleistocene greenhouse/lab where he considers what to do. Cassie comes to talk with him as Alex paces, staring out at a projected prehistoric landscape. They discuss the impact of resurrected species on native animals. Mammoths have taken their former place among the caribou and musk ox with which they shared these lands in the last Ice Age. However, in such a new environment with so many variables, some resurrected species may be breeding and succeeding far better than they hoped. Cassie is concerned that this could lead to unusual population pressures, fierce competition among diverse predators and specific prey. Her surveys and analyses are doubly important now. It is imperative that they gather the necessary data.

Alex cares about her very much, and his ability to maintain a strictly business face in front of her is fading. The barrier begins to break down—and then Zach enters with some routine news. The moment is lost. More and more, Zach translates his frustration at not getting Cassie into envy toward Alex.

The violent protesters are sure to attack other mammoth feed stockpiles, but Alex knows he can't call in law enforcement against either Gregor Galaev or against the Evos (*that* much was proven in the aftermath of the Montana attack). Alex distrusts Federal authorities and knows he is *on his own now.*

One of Alex's early genetic-engineering patents had involved a way to protect humans from "Montezuma's Revenge" and other forms of diarrhea. However, the Defense Department had also courted Helyx Corp, trying to convince him to create biological "irritants," tailoring such organisms to attack people in everything from dirty-tricks government operations to outright warfare. But Alex had refused all such contracts, but now he unlocks his old "biological closet" and finds samples of just such a tailored bacterium, nicknamed Montezuma Junior. This will be very unpleasant for humans, but harmless to mammoths. Alex reassures Cassie that he doesn't want to hurt anyone, but this microorganism will be enough to make the vile saboteurs miserable.

In showcase zoos around the world, the Japanese-bred dwarf mammoths begin to die from their insidious disease. Most zoos have quarantined the once-extinct animals, and public unrest grows heated. There has already been a near riot in Munich at the old Olympic grounds where two of the mini-mammoths were on display.

Sylvia Chesney receives alarming reports and images from a triumphant-sounding Senator Karl Fitch. Preliminary analysis of samples from the dead dwarf mammoths has indicated that the animals do indeed suffer from a previously unknown retrovirus. What if it can jump across species lines and infect humans, just as Kinsman and the Evos had feared?

Maybe this is something to worry about after all … maybe something she can use. Sylvia agrees to allow Senator Fitch to summon Alex Pierce in for closed-door meeting in Washington, DC.

Kinsman and his Evo saboteurs break into the Preserve to cause more mischief, to burn more food depots. This time, though, they unwittingly trigger the booby-traps Alex has set for them. As they try to set a fire, they are suddenly sprayed with a cloying mist. Choking, Kinsman and his cohorts scramble to retreat, wondering what the awful scientist has done to them.

Later, the Evos have to dash off into the bushes, each of them afflicted with Montezuma Junior.

Cassie and Alex have set up a small expedition to the northern section of the Preserve, where they will complete a survey of the sabretooth population: marking the cats, recording their habits, and taking a census of their population. It is a vital scientific mission, but it will also be a special time for the two of them, though neither will admit it.

He and Cassie are ready to go, fully armed with high-tech equipment, GPS locators, and a fast chopter. Then Alex receives word from his lawyer Randall LeVay about the news of the retrovirus found in the dwarf mammoths. The Senate Committee has summoned him to Washington DC and speak on behalf of the Resurrection Preserve. LeVay is fighting the summons, using every legal strategy he can devise, but Alex is confident he can sway the politicians.

He will have to assign Cassie a pilot and send her north to complete her studies without him. Alex is concerned about her going alone, but she has done this half a dozen times before, especially with her Library of Earth work. Cassie is very independent and better able to handle herself than most ranch hands. The chopter and mobile labs are all packed, and she is ready to depart for the northern security zone. Alex heads to Washington, where he will face a battle as fierce as a mammoth fighting a sabretooth. He must save the Preserve.

✦   ✦   ✦

With Alex and Cassie both gone, now Zach Browder—left in charge of running the day-to-day operations of the Preserve—goes to Gregor's private compound.

Zach has been taking bribes from Gregor for some time now, looking the other way while some of Gregor's people slip into the preserve to harvest the narcotic ferns, to snatch a few dire wolves or occasional exotic species. The mammoth slaughter, though, went beyond the bounds. Never before has he particularly cared what Gregor did.

Though Zach has been Alex's close employee for many years, he is like a resentful assistant who justifies embezzling company property, convincing himself that he *deserves* a salary more in keeping with his boss's. He still holds to his environmentalist ideals, but thinks himself more realistic now. He has been taking money under the table from Gregor, sure that he's "just getting his due, not really hurting anybody."

The loss of one mammoth should have been no big deal, especially not for a richer-than-God businessman like Alex. Since mammoths in the wild would be culled by predators and diseases anyway, Zach had convinced himself that a single animal would not be an unacceptable loss. Though his motives aren't as pure as Cassie's, Zach does care for the animals, has vague ideals for protecting endangered species. But seeing the bloody mess and cruel ineptitude of Gregor's hunters pissed him off. "That butchery was inexcusable!" He appeals to Gregor's hunting sensibility, which actually sinks in.

Now Gregor is all charm and charisma, apologizing for the incompetence of his underlings and says he will reprimand the man who showed such poor judgment. Perhaps he will assign the clods to work on miserable fishing boats high in the Arctic Sea.

Gregor doesn't want to lose Zach's cooperation, especially now that he is starting to set up a distribution system for the psychotropic Pleistocene ferns. He reassures Zach that from now on, his people will only harvest some of the rare plants growing wild in the high meadows, and slip back out again. Zach grudgingly agrees, so long as it never goes beyond that.

A group of Gregor's henchmen (without Psyk) slips through the Preserve fences and harvest big sacks of the curling ferns, then races back toward the boundary on their snow-skimmers.

When they enter the forest near the fence, however, they are surrounded and attacked by a pack of black dire wolves. These are ferocious predators, heavily muscled, with long teeth and powerful jaws. Thought to have died out after Alex reintroduced them to the Preserve, some of the dire wolves have interbred with native wolves, resulting in a very successful hybrid.

Gregor's drug-runners try to defend themselves, but the dire wolves are smart, and cooperate, picking them off one by one. Only after the last man is dead does the pack begin to feast.

Suffering from Montezuma Jr., Kinsman and the Evos stumble across the Preserve wilderness trying to get to their pickup point. En route, though, the ailing eco-terrorists come upon the massacre site where the dire wolves have killed Gregor's drug runners. They encounter the wrecked snowskimmers and the torn and unrecognizable bodies.

Among the carnage, Kinsman discovers sacks of harvested psychotropic ferns and wonders what these people could have been doing … and what predator killed them. Drugs, dangerous animals … Kinsman smiles. Exactly the kind of evidence he has been looking for.

He takes numerous images of the bloody scene, the mangled faces, the gutted bodies. Then he uploads them to a satellite receiver, knowing that these pictures will strike a more significant blow to Helyx Corp than the destruction of the Montana ranch.

Flying with one of the competent Helyx pilots Cassie goes into the northern wilderness of the Resurrection Preserve. She spends the day flying around at work, doing her species tally. Landing frequently, she walks among the muskox and caribou, counting mammoths, studying evidence of sabretooths (footprints, droppings), taking samples.

However, when the pilot tries to use the radio to transmit a report to Zach Browder, the radio won't work. "We're being jammed. What the hell?" With a whine and a pop, the chopter engine dies as if it has just been switched off. Even the static from the radio falls silent, all electronic systems gone dead. The chopter has been whomped by a powerful microwave pulse.

Out of control, the pilot wrestles with the chopter, which is falling like a rock out of the sky. At the pilot's urging, Cassie bails out into thick snow. Then the chopter crashes into thick trees, killing the pilot and destroying the aircraft, the radio, their supplies.

Cassie picks herself up, shaken. Without a vehicle, without her sonic fence, without even a radio or a weapon, she is stranded and completely cut off—alone in a predator-filled wilderness....

Proud and confident, Gregor Galaev hosts a grand hunt at his estate. This is what he's been wanting all along—to start taking advantage of the Pleistocene treasure trove from the Preserve. He invites only his most special clients, including Hector Chu and Uruk Bey (the Samarkand clan leader who purchased his own breeding pair of dire wolves). Gregor shows them a cage containing a ravenous and ferocious sabretooth tiger, stolen from the Resurrection Preserve.

Zach Browder is there, making sure everything is done properly. All the high-end hunters are armed and equipped. This will be the first-ever hunt of modern man against a sabretooth, a history-making event. The sabretooth is turned loose, bounding out into the confines of the large compound. The dogs are sent after it. Eager hunters set out on the chase.

In the closed-door session in Washington, Alex defends himself. He admits there is some possibility that woolly mammoths originally went extinct because of a disease … mammoth AIDS? He dismisses rumors about the unusual Pleistocene allergies some workers have experienced on his preserve.

LeVay does a good job keeping the inquiries on track, sticking to the legalities. Both men know that pressure is mounting, and that powerful forces are trying to shut down the Resurrection Preserve. The Committee Senators ask Alex many rapid-fire antagonistic questions. "What sort of Frankenstein horrors are you creating with your genetic research up there?" "Why do you arrogantly refuse to allow inspectors?" Some Senators are more concerned that Alex is not paying his "proper share" of taxes, since he has poured all his income into "donations" to ecological organizations.

Then scowling Senator Fitch springs on him the shocking images of the murdered henchmen found on his preserve—Kinsman's photos. "These were transmitted directly to the Committee."

Alex is flabbergasted, knowing nothing about this. Remembering Zach Browder's report of the mangled Kodiak bear, Alex cannot deny the clear evidence that dangerous animals must be loose on the Preserve. Now that dead bodies have been found, there must be an immediate investigation. LeVay tries stalling the Committee, but Alex cuts him off. "Murders were committed. We can't deny the investigators." Sylvia will put together an inspection team from her committee and they will be at the Resurrection Preserve within two days.

Alex departs immediately.

✦　　✦　　✦

Cut off from outside contact, Cassie spends the night beside a blazing campfire. She has scavenged a few items from the chopter wreckage, buried the dead pilot, even nursed a burning branch from the crash so that she could keep a fire going. Always intrigued by the sabretooth tigers, she now feels a primal fear rush through her as the massive feline predators roar in the night, just outside the range of her firelight. She sleeps huddled inside the dubious shelter of the burned shell of the chopter.

A powerful tawny shape emerges from the darkness and slams into the vehicle, rocking it and leaving a large dent. With a sound like fingernails on a chalkboard, the big sabretooth rakes claws across the fuselage. But he can't get inside. The sabretooth disappears back into the night shadows and waits....

Cassie knows she won't last another night like this. The chopter is mangled, and the big cats could probably break in if they tried again. The next morning, she scribbles a note and leaves it in the cockpit wreckage.

Then, armed only with a scavenged pistol, a compass, and a topo map, she begins her long walk across the Resurrection Preserve, stalked by sabretooths.

With plenty of tense action, Gregor's hand-picked big-game hunters track the frenzied cat. The sabretooth kills one of the hunters, using its long fangs to rip open his throat and leaves him to bleed on the hunting grounds, which shakes up the remaining hunters. Gregor is not bothered—this is, after all, survival of the fittest.

While pursued, the big cat doubles back and surprisingly returns to the well-lit estate house, where Gregor's daughter Raisa has been told to remain inside, guarded by Psyk's son Nikolai. Gregor's henchman Yuri (the loose-cannon who botched the mammoth-tusk hunt) has remained in the house, too, and makes a foolish mistake (leaves a door or window open), and the sabretooth gets inside the house and almost kills Raisa.

Trained as a hunter by his father, Nikolai defends Raisa with his own knife, bravely fighting the monstrous prehistoric cat. He kills it, but is himself mortally wounded. He dies even as Psyk and the hunters rush in. Psyk wails in grief.

PART III—SURVIVAL OF THE FITTEST

When Alex returns from his grilling in Washington, he makes preparations for the arrival of Senator Chesney's investigative team. Randall LeVay comes along to brief the ranch personnel and to look over their operations from a legal perspective.

Those concerns vanish in an instant, though, when Alex learns that Cassie hasn't checked in. Zach has just returned from Gregor's disastrous sabretooth hunt and is surprised that Alex is back already. He has just noticed that Cassie and the pilot did not check in as expected. Now, when Zach tries to contact her, he gets no response.

Normally, Alex would be confident that she can take care of herself, but now he has a strong, uneasy feeling. In no uncertain terms, Alex orders Zach to take him in another chopter. He leaves LeVay at the Preserve headquarters to take care of matters. "Senator Chesney be damned. I'm going to find Cassie and make sure she's all right."

During daylight, Cassie trudges along, leaving clear trail markings in case anyone comes to follow her. She has never been one to sit around and wait for help, though she hopes in her heart that Alex will come to rescue her.

In a clearing, she comes upon a herd of magnificent woolly mammoths. Filled with wonder, she watches them. One of the big bulls uses his long, curved tusks like a shovel to clear away snow and expose vegetation underneath. *(This is a controversial theory about mammoth behavior, based on the most current research.)*

Cassie then watches the grazing mammoths as they seek out the weird psychotropic ferns—but when they eat the ferns, the beasts get frisky, then seem to go completely loco. Bull mammoths charge each other in a titanic battle, smashing thick skulls, clashing tusks like knights in a jousting tournament.

Cassie slips away from the primal duel, frightened by the ferocity she has witnessed, and wonders what could possibly be in those ferns....

After the horrible death of Nikolai, Gregor sends Raisa back to her mother in far-off Moscow. Though distraught over the loss of her friend, she wants to stay in Alaska, but Gregor insists. Psyk stands beside them, stiff as a statue.

Gregor has just received a call from Senator Chesney, knows that she and her team are on their way to investigate the Resurrection Preserve. Raisa wants to see her buddy Sylvia, but Gregor puts her on the airplane. He must keep his daughter safe, and he knows that now things will get very ugly, very soon, and he does not want his daughter around. This is what he has been waiting for, and he knows that Alex will soon be out of the picture entirely.

✦   ✦   ✦

Taking their chopter, Zach and Alex discover Cassie's crash site far in the northern wilderness. They find her message and the buried pilot, so they know she is still alive. "We're going to have to track her." The two men set out to follow Cassie's trail, noting the blaze marks on trees, footprints in the snow.

On her survival trek, Cassie shoots at the stalking sabretooths, reluctant to kill the animals she has worked so hard to nurture and breed, but finally she has no choice but to take one down as it charges her. The others don't slow down at all. She scrambles up a tree, trying to get high enough that the cats will leave her alone, but they begin climbing after her. Things look very bad for Cassie.

Then Alex and Zach arrive, yelling and shooting to scare the big cats away. Cassie finally takes a shot at the closest big male on the branches climbing toward her. She barely nicks it with her bullet, but the noise startles it enough that the cat tumbles off the branch. The sabretooth limps away, snarling.

Hungry, cold, scared, and bedraggled, Cassie is reunited with Alex. He embraces her—then backs away in embarrassment. She grabs him and delivers a powerful kiss. Overjoyed, he feels as if he could take on anything now.

Zach sees this sudden shift between them and can barely control his frustration. Super-rich Alex has won *again....*

After the debacle of the hunt, Gregor takes his nervous henchman Yuri aside, choosing an appropriate punishment. Yuri made the inexcusable mistake of letting the hunted animal get inside, endangering Raisa, killing Psyk's son. He leads Yuri into a room facing two doors. "Have you ever heard the story about the Lady or the Tiger?" Behind one door is another terrible sabretooth and certain death, behind the other door is just a man. Yuri must choose.

He is about to open one of the doors when behind it he hears a quiet rustle, a growl, and he immediately chooses the other door, sure he has avoided the tiger. He pulls open the door to find a grim and bloodthirsty Psyk holding a .45. Psyk brings up the pistol in a fast, smooth motion and shoots Yuri in the head. As the man falls to the floor, Psyk keeps firing until he has emptied the clip, but still his anger isn't satisfied. Gregor is safely out of range of the flying blood. "We may as well feed his body to the sabretooth anyway."

That night Alex and Cassie finally make love. They hold each other, at last brought together by the ominous events and the ordeal they have just been through. Finally released, they are desperate to find comfort in each other. Part of Alex is still deeply saddened by the tragedy of his murdered wife, and always will be, but he cannot deny his feelings for Cassie.

Alex created the whole Resurrection Preserve, and the genetic Library of Earth, to honor Helen's dreams, and Cassie has devoted her life to those mammoths and to saving endangered species. Together, they worked so hard to recreate a snapshot of the Pleistocene Era, and they are on the verge of succeeding—except for the intervention of short-sighted modern humans. Now, through politics instead of overhunting, the humans want to make these precious creatures extinct all over again.

Cassie sleeps softly beside him, but Alex stays awake long into the night....

The exhibition mini-mammoths in Tokyo grow visibly sick. Dying, they are taken from public view. But Evo protesters are concerned about the possible spread of a prehistoric retrovirus. A riot breaks out in the Japan facility, and the dwarf mammoths are all killed by a mob. The Japanese chief researcher, who was once Alex's rival, is helpless to stop it.

Senator Chesney's team arrives in Alaska. She expertly milks the media, promising that her team will leave no stone unturned.

Gregor welcomes them, a fine diplomat and host, and escorts them out to his own facility near the Resurrection Preserve. He drops subtle hints that, while he himself is a businessman helping the economy of Alaska and trying to strengthen ties with neighboring Siberia, Alex Pierce is an obsessive loose-cannon, intent on research for its own sake without grasping the consequences.

Playing the good host in his big house, Gregor serves Sylvia, grumpy Senator Fitch, the Surgeon General, and their aides a banquet of roast passenger pigeon—a meal no human has eaten for a century or more. When someone asks why he would kill the once-extinct birds he fought so hard to bring back, he explains that the Preserve is still a testing ground, that the ecosystems are in flux, and that he has no choice but to keep the bird population in check. And if any irregularities are found, any shred of evidence of genuine prehistoric plagues, then he will insist the whole place be quarantined and all future work stopped.

Gregor believes he is orchestrating events. The reader suspects, though, that Sylvia is adroitly using him instead, relying on Gregor's genuine affection for her. She lets Senator Fitch take the extreme Evo position, positioning herself as the moderate. We see her setting Gregor up for a fall.

Ominously, someone sneezes—Pleistocene hay fever again—and the investigation team looks as if they've already made up their minds.

The Senate investigation team flies to the Resurrection Preserve, where they are met by a cooperative Alex. They head out into the field, guided by Alex and Cassie, with Zach riding along for security.

Kinsman and his Evos (by now recovered from the miserable Montezuma Junior infection) are sure that it is time to take overt action to crush the Preserve. He has secret orders, and now the Evos will take matters into their own hands.

Kinsman stalks the mammoths near where the team is going to visit. He has a long rifle and darts filled with enough stimulant to madden an entire herd of cattle … or one woolly mammoth. As the Senate team approaches the herd, Kinsman shoots the nearest big bull, jolting it with enough chemicals to enrage it. Then he slips back into the forest, his work completed.

Cassie leads the Senate team in closer to the mammoths, hoping the politicians will see the wonder that she does. It is the Resurrection Preserve's only chance. She has walked among the russet mammoths many times. The investigators are filled with wonder to see the majestic creatures first hand. Alex beams with pride, thinking that everything might turn out all right after all.

Suddenly, one of the largest bulls becomes a rogue and goes on a rampage. Cassie wants to intervene, but Alex sees how wild the mammoth is and he drags her away. Gregor Galaev grabs Sylvia, then takes care of himself.

The crazed mammoth kills Senator Fitch in a gruesome manner, goring him with a long tusk and then stomping him to paste. Finally, Zach and Psyk bring down the rogue mammoth with a heavy volley of well-placed shots.

[Here we throw the reader a curve. Until now, Fitch has been the political figure who always sides with the Evo position. The reader doesn't like him, and thus he also acts as a red herring: the reader will assume that

Kinsman's secret and powerful benefactor is Fitch. His death apparently clears the field of support for Kinsman, distracting the reader from who is truly behind Kinsman.]

In stunned horror, the survivors flee back toward the protection of the main Preserve buildings. All of this occurs as live media feeds transmit images to a worldwide audience.

✦ ✦ ✦

Alex is completely disgraced—it's his Preserve, even if the visit wasn't his idea. The stunned Senator Chesney immediately calls in her standby National Guard troops to oversee the shutdown of the Resurrection Preserve. Alex is arrested for gross negligence, reckless endangerment, and a host of other charges. He is taken away to prison under armed military escort. Randall LeVay, is already working on appeals and injunctions, but Alex doesn't think they'll have enough time for the legal system to grind through their options.

Cassie is in despair, but not surprised when Alex receives a Federal order from the Surgeon General, backed up by a Presidential condemnation: "All Helyx workers and Preserve employees are to be removed from the ranch and quarantined, until such time as medical tests have verified that they are no risk for spreading the prehistoric retrovirus."

This is the Resurrection Preserve's darkest hour.

PART IV—PLEISTOCENE RULES

Inside the armed camp of the Resurrection Preserve, Gregor Galaev comes to Senator Chesney with an idea that he believes will be most satisfying. He knows that she intends to impound many of Alex's assets, a scheme they cooked up together, and Gregor will get the rest of the Resurrection Preserve. They have both seized the opportunity that the mammoth attack has offered.

Now Gregor sees a tremendous opportunity. The sabretooth hunt was the merest prelude—he wants to hold a high-priced and secret event for his most special customers: the first *mammoth hunt* in recorded history. His chosen big-game hunters can have the thrill of their lives.

Ambitious, knowing that this plot could not have been pulled off without Gregor's behind-the-scenes cooperation, Sylvia agrees. If the mammoths—in fact, all of the formerly extinct animals—should happen to be designated "a menace to the human race," perhaps they could sell extremely expensive hunting permits for bounty hunters to go into the Preserve. Gregor secretly has his own embryo samples in Siberia and is willing to continue the operation there.

Zach is uneasy to be caught in the middle of the debacle. He was in charge of security here, but now he has no role at all. Gregor says, "We will have a new job for you in the next couple of days, Mr. Browder. As a hunting guide."

With a sparkle in his eye, Gregor then sets his most interesting condition. This mammoth hunt will be conducted just as it was by our ancestors—without modern equipment, or high-tech tracking devices, or powerful automatic weapons. All hunters must agree to abide by *Pleistocene Rules*: spears and wits, man against mammoth.

Senator Chesney is surprised, but the wheels are turning in her mind. She agrees to let him plan the hunt, though she wonders who would want to do such a thing. Gregor just smiles at her. He doesn't doubt for a second that he will have more takers than he can handle.

Randall LeVay is trying to get Alex released on bail (he's got billions), to appeal the charges, to do anything to postpone the drastic government action.

Finally, since Alex is not deemed much of a flight risk, the judge sets bail of a million dollars, which should be easily met by the wealthy corporate president. Alex tells LeVay to pay the amount right away—then the lawyer is astonished to find that all of Helyx Corp's assets have been frozen, thanks to trumped-up RICO charges that Senator Chesney has filed. Alex doesn't have access to a penny of his fortune. He's still stuck in jail.

In the deserted main house of the Resurrection Preserve, sleeping in the private quarters where she made love with Alex, a distraught Cassie discovers a secret storage area containing more frozen genetic samples. The vials are labeled "HELEN." An icy shock runs up her spine. Has he been intending to clone his wife once the technology was developed? Or was this just a thread of hope he clung to in his despair? She holds the samples, her heart torn.

Then Kinsman and his Evos break into the main lab and systematically destroy the precious genetic samples carefully preserved as the Library of Earth. It reminds her all too much of the raid on the Montana ranch, the night Helen was killed. She frantically tries to stop them, but the Evos have done their damage and disappear into the night. The main house is in flames.

Racing into the Preserve's control room, Cassie shuts down all of the sonic perimeter fences, secretly deactivating the electronic barricades that surround the Preserve. She hopes that some of the once-extinct animals will escape to the far north. Maybe even to Siberia, over pack ice.

Gregor and his picked hunters (Uruk Bey, Hector Chu, etc.) go out in a grand expedition. Psyk also accompanies them, still distraught from the death of his son. The party sets up camp, ready for the adventure of their lives. These are tough customers, poachers and powerful men who have no respect for laws. Sylvia Chesney is part of the group, though it is doubtful she will do any hunting herself—she wants to be beside Gregor (and to look for her opportunity). Zach Browder will ride ahead as a scout for the party, tracking down the mammoths.

Though the hunt will ostensibly follow "Pleistocene Rules," using only primitive weapons, the hunters have brought along enough surreptitious firepower to take out an army. The skies and grounds are mercifully free of media snoops. Gregor knows this will be the greatest hunt he has ever experienced. His private footage alone, shot by microcams, will be worth a fortune in the media.

Surprisingly, Alex's million-dollar bail is paid. Nobody expected this, and even the judge is astonished. LeVay is amazed, but quickly leads his boss out of jail. They learn that the money has been offered by the head of the Japanese group, Alex's former rival. The message says only, "You fight for all of us."

LeVay warns Alex about the strict conditions of the bail. "You are not allowed to leave Alaska, or even the vicinity." Alex gives his lawyer a grim smile. "Going away from the Preserve is the opposite of what I intend to do."

On his snow-skimmer, Zach scouts ahead of Gregor's hunting group. He is still aching from Cassie's rejection. She knows about the hunt Gregor has proposed and hates Zach for taking part in it so easily. He heads north in search of the main mammoth herd, though the surreptitious hunters already have a good idea of the location, thanks to the Preserve's security monitors. The hunting party will follow in jeeps until they locate the herd, then they will set up camp, using thermal tents and fancy wilderness gear.

Gregor and Psyk watch the big-game hunters at their campsite in the mid-afternoon. Uruk Bey and Hector Chu ineffectually throw spears made from saplings fitted with stone points—they can't seem to hit the broad side of a mammoth. When Psyk throws his spears, he hits the target every time.

As night falls, the wind picks up and the weather turns very cold. Senator Chesney gets a satellite update and learns about a big blizzard coming in from the Pacific, which will dump a lot of snow over the Preserve.

Gregor tries to reassure her. "In the last Ice Age, survival depended on hunting mammoths. Men had to go out, risk their lives, never mind the weather—or the tribe did not eat. Are we less than they were? Tomorrow humans will hunt mammoths again for the first time in 10,000 years."

Sylvia, though, seems concerned about something more than just weather.

Free on bail, Alex slips back inside his Preserve. He uses his knowledge of the place and also how to thwart his own defensive systems. Although he allowed Zach to control the surveillance and security, Alex is sufficiently embittered by the Montana assault that he doesn't quite trust anybody.

Inside, he meets up with Cassie and is appalled to see the destroyed main house, the wrecked Library of Earth ... and, worse, the illicit mammoth hunt.

He knows Gregor is behind it, but since the Senator is herself cooperating, he has no recourse by normal means to stop it. He has been disgraced, the mammoths given a death sentence anyway, and he no longer has any credibility in the public eye. Alex doesn't understand what forces are being arrayed against him, but he must find some way to stop the destruction of everything he has worked for. Arming themselves, putting on survival gear, Alex and Cassie go together into the Pleistocene wilderness.

Next morning, under gloomy gray skies and a freshening wind that whips stinging ice particles into the air, the hunters set out with a party atmosphere.

Some of the hunters show off their bravado, but Gregor knows this is deadly serious. Brainstorming like men at a corporate board meeting, the hunters have developed a plan to surround the animals and cut off a few members. But as they proceed with their scheme, the men have no real experience, and the hunt rapidly begins to go wrong. (This will be an ironic counterpoint to the dramatized Pleistocene hunt in the prologue.)

Psyk, the only truly competent hunter in the group (other than Gregor), rushes in among the mammoths with his spear. Psyk himself is pumped up on the wild fern-drug. He feels he is part of the forest, connected with the mammoths. He seems completely separate from the rest of the sportsmen, focused on his prey, just like the old ways, just like he has experienced in his visions. Psyk selects his target, ignoring the shouts, the other running people.

He has a deep spiritual link with this great beast. The spear is hard and strong in his hand. He comes forward, bends back his arm, and *knows* where and when to throw. His weapon strikes true, deep into the vulnerable neck. The mammoth bellows and falls. Psyk knows this is the way the hunt must be—not a rich man's game, but a communion.

But the inexperienced hunters only panic the remaining beasts. Even as Psyk's kill falls to the snowy, trampled meadow, a flurry of misplaced spears flies all over the place, missing targets, bouncing off of thick woolly hides. The rest of the mammoths rally in a surprisingly organized fashion and begin to stampede *toward* the hunters, not away.

In the total chaos, most of the puny humans dodge into a dense stand of trees—safe, but humiliated. Psyk, though, gets separated from the group (not entirely by accident, since he's reveling in this). He stays behind in the wild.

✦   ✦   ✦

Dusk. Back in camp, scared and confused and full of second thoughts, some of the big-game hunters want to pull out. This is too much! Hector Chu wants to take their modern weapons, go back to kick some mammoth butt.

But night is falling, and the storm worsens. The hunters bed down in comfort, though they remain restless. Not caring about appearances, especially not in this bunch, Sylvia Chesney shares her tent and sleeping bag with Gregor.

Then, out of the thickening blizzard come the mammoths, marching with an eerie intelligence. The big animals know where the poachers are and seem to understand that these humans are the enemy. In the last Ice Age, mammoths and humans co-evolved, learning how to survive against each other, and these newly resurrected specimens have some of those ancient instincts.

Gregor gets out of the tent just before the big beasts smash the equipment (including their communications equipment and locators). The Senator suffers a broken wrist and a deep gash to her thigh. Hector Chu is tangled up in his sleeping bag. Some of the more cool-headed hunters scramble through the smashed and scattered equipment, searching for weapons. Gregor and Uruk Bey light torches and drive the mammoths back with the bright fire.

The damage done, the behemoths rumble off into the darkness.

In the aftermath of the attack, with their camp in ruins, Gregor tries to figure out what to do. His affair with Sylvia has touched him more deeply than he expected. He goes to her tent to make her more comfortable and overhears her talking on a secret transmitter demanding an immediate pickup:

"The response team has got to come in and make the strike now. I know we've got the Evos in place, but they're fuckups—can't count on them at all. No, I don't care about the blizzard!"

Gregor hears a military voice answer her: "The aircraft and assault teams will arrive first thing in the morning, if the skies are clear. Kinsman has been requesting backup too—" She loses control and shouts into her mike, "Forget them! They've botched enough simple tasks already."

Gregor suddenly understands—*Sylvia* is the force behind the Evos, who have been violent gadflies against Alex's work all along. Previously, he knew and supported her plans to grab the Resurrection Preserve, but he did not suspect the extent of her machinations.

When he confronts her, Sylvia kisses him and admits that she has long intended to close down the politically unpopular Resurrection Preserve, championing an issue big enough to keep herself in the news. In addition, if she can confiscate Helyx's assets, it will be a multibillion-dollar prize! She was using the Clean Genes activists, of course, but the Federal forces she is calling in were another suit in her hand.

Although Sylvia has been in cahoots with him, Gregor always believed that *he* was using *her*. Now he wonders just how far she will go.

After the mammoth attack, the big-game hunters tensely wait for daylight.

With the first light of dawn, Zach is dispatched on their lone snow-skimmer to fetch help from Gregor's estate. He takes an assault rifle for protection.

Hector Chu proudly reveals that he has hidden a powerful Magnum pistol inside his warm jacket. That should be enough firepower to protect them until the Senator's military help can pick them up.

Gregor looks around the damaged camp, and a cold smile crosses his face. He takes one of the spears and gathers his warm clothes, gloves, boots, hunting knife. Sensing the testosterone in the air, Uruk Bey asks him what he is doing. Gregor says, "I came to hunt a mammoth. I intend to do it."

Approaching the hunters' encampment, Cassie and Alex know that these people are their enemies. They look with some satisfaction at what the mammoths have done. "We've got some unexpected Pleistocene allies," she says, then sees Zach depart on his snowskimmer.

Alex sees Gregor leaving on his own, obsessed with his hunt. Alex considers the Siberian godfather to be the root of all his problems. Scowling, he tells Cassie to head off Zach farther down the trail and enlist his aid out of sight of the other hunters. Meanwhile, he intends to face Gregor—alone.

Moving through the trees, Cassie races to intercept Zach on his way to the Preserve's central compound. She almost makes it in time. As Zach passes, Cassie tries to get his attention, but with the humming engine, he can't hear her shout. As he departs, Cassie stands with her hands on her hips, wondering what to do now. Then she hears a sound behind her and turns to confront a pack of hungry dire wolves. The predators have stalked and cornered her, and there are far too many of them for the few bullets she has in her rifle.

Cassie starts shooting.

Separated from the other Evos by the storm, Kinsman is ready to accomplish a lot on his own. From high ground, looking down at the agitated mammoth herd, he thinks about how much he hates the beasts. He has despised Helyx for bringing back extinct misfits that have no business in the modern world … and he hates Alex for ruining his career. He takes out his powerful new weapons—given to him by Senator Chesney's friends in high places.

Kinsman starts shooting at the mammoths below. He puts several down with explosive rounds and wounds many more of the animals. He keeps firing. It feels right—just as it did back in Montana.

And then he sees a much more gratifying target.…

Out in the snowy forests, close to the mammoth herd, Alex meets up with Gregor Galaev. He is furious at what the Siberian has done. The slaughter of the first mammoth and now this reckless hunt. The two men stand in the open, both knowing that they have always been meant to settle the issue this way—not with lawyers and memos and board meetings, but here, in a primitive state.

In the howling wind, both men want blood. They circle each other, flinging accusations. Though both are leaders, used to directing others to do the dangerous jobs, neither man is a warrior. Alex uses his fists, and the fight worsens. They roll down a steep slope, crack through the ice in a shallow, half-frozen stream. Alex and Gregor come up drenched and freezing, but with knives at each other's throats. Alex curses Gregor for what he has done to the wonderful Resurrection work, to the dream his wife Helen had.

Gregor in turn accuses Alex of bringing the ruin down upon himself—for being blind to the public, never thinking of the consequences of his work, just loving it for its own sake. They could have had a wonderful preserve, restoring extinct animals, maintaining the Library of Earth, allowing an occasional hunt to make the preserve profitable—all possible, if only Alex had been more careful!

Then they hear gunshots. The mammoth herd bellows. They watch as several of the beasts are taken down. "You and your damned hunters!" Alex cries. Gregor sees the shooter—Kinsman—and says, "That's not one of them."

Then Kinsman spots them and opens fire, high-caliber, explosive bullets chewing up the snow and trees around them. Alex and Gregor run for cover.

Zach Browder, on his way for help, hears Cassie's rifle shots behind him.

He spins his skimmer around, spraying snow, and races back to investigate. He comes upon Cassie cornered by the dire wolves. They are circling, harrying her. Three wolves are already dead, but she is running out of ammunition. Her left side has been clawed and torn, bleeding.

Zach doesn't say a word. He loves this woman, despite all the pain she has caused him. He comes in on his snow-skimmer, scatters some of the wolves, then climbs off the vehicle, taking out his rifle and shooting several more. While the dire wolves regroup, he urges Cassie to get on the vehicle. The wolves come in again, snarling, full of fangs.

Moving slowly because of her injury, Cassie climbs onto the snow-skimmer. Zach shoots another wolf, but two more jump onto his back, bearing him down. The other wolves mob him. Cassie tries to shoot, but her rifle is out of ammunition. Two wolves leap at her, and she swings her rifle, smacking one wolf in the muzzle with the stock.

Zach is already dead. She has no choice but to streak away on the snow-skimmer, her arms stiff, her entire body tensed and clenched.

The dire wolves howl after her in the forest.

At the wrecked camp, the wounded Sylvia Chesney waits with Hector Chu. The Chinese businessman holds his magnum like a crucifix to ward off vampires, as if the very sight of it will scare away predators.

A small group of sabretooths approaches the camp, stalking them. The Senator is sure that they can smell the blood from her injuries. Seeing the flash of tawny fur, the rippling panther-like bodies, Hector Chu fires his magnum—and the recoil bowls him over into the snow. The bullet hits a tree trunk ten feet from his target, but the sabretooth bolts anyway.

The Senator knows the animals will be back. She is cold and in pain and very surly. "What an ass!" She looks at the Chinese businessman. "Haven't you fired that thing before?" Hector confesses that he hasn't.

Out in the snow, Gregor and Alex—unlikely allies now—try to deal with Kinsman, who has turned back to slaughtering the mammoths. Alex has a score to settle with Kinsman. Gregor understands what they both need to do.

"We are fools," he says. Alex nods. "You bet."

Though the blizzard has abated somewhat, the snow is still coming down. Wary now, the mammoths smell the approaching humans and grow very alert. They have already attacked the encampment and now they are agitated, defending their turf against these new hunters.

The mammoths demonstrate advanced cooperative behavior—a clear sign that they could adapt to human hunting patterns, but were made extinct by a combination of climate changes, diseases, and human hunting. Some of the beasts take up defensive positions, while other herd members begin to search for a way up the steep hill, to where the sniper is hidden.

Kinsman is so focused on the odd behavior of the mammoths that Alex and Gregor are able to sneak up behind him in the blizzard. Working together, Alex distracts the terrorist. As Kinsman stands up to shoot at him, Gregor smacks him with a tree branch, disarming the man.

Holding the weapon on him, Alex knows that the Evos were not acting independently. Kinsman confesses that Senator Chesney was giving him orders.

They are suddenly startled when several mammoths crash into the clearing, stalking the sniper, not discriminating among the humans. Kinsman uses the diversion to bolt into the thickening snowstorm, while Alex and Gregor also flee.

Psyk looks like a wild man now after the violent mammoth hunt and then spending the night out in the forest. He remembers hunting with his son Nikolai. In one of the snowy bogs, he cracks the thin film of ice to get at the tender nubs of growing ferns beneath. He eats the psychotropic ferns raw, chewing slowly, feeling the drug suffuse his body. A Pleistocene high.

Barely able to see ahead of him in the thick falling snow, Kinsman runs. His breath comes in gasps. He hopes he can link up with the rest of the Evos. If he can arrange to leave with Sylvia's response team secretly backing them, he'll go into hiding. Since he got off from the murder and mayhem at the Montana mammoth ranch, why should this be any different?

He checks his map, taking bearings via a global positioning satellite. He is not worried … until he discovers that he is in a wind-whipped meadow among giant shadowy shapes, hulking woolly behemoths with enormous curved tusks. He has blundered into the middle of the mammoths he was shooting.

The huge bulls twitch their trunks, touching the big mounds of carcasses—the animals Kinsman has slain. The mammoths know he is there. They stand eerily silent, like totems in the blizzard. But as they begin to shift and form a circle, he realizes they have surrounded him. Intentionally.

The mammoths close in, smart and vengeful. They have cut off Kinsman's escape in all directions. They raise their trunks and trumpet into the blanketing white silence, a soaring cry that strikes primal fear deep into his bones.

Mr. Clean Genes soils his jeans. He doesn't even have a chance to run.

Heading back toward the hunters' camp, outwitting the mammoths that have nearly killed them, Alex and Gregor are in turmoil. Gregor may be a romantic beneath his shell, but he is a genius at the dynamics of power. He now understands that Sylvia has meant to destroy *both* him and Alex.

On top of shutting down the Preserve and confiscating Helyx's assets, Sylvia can also deliver the notorious former Soviet mafia boss "Gregor Galaev." Many Federal agencies, starting with the CIA, will be ecstatic. Using Gregor and Alex as scapegoats, with evidence of the drug running from the Preserve, the Senator will use RICO laws to grab everything. The huge public benefit she will reap from all this is sure to put her in the governor's mansion.

Gregor has been a fool. And all of it coming from his deepest vulnerability—a woman as clever as he. He will have to become an exile again as soon as the authorities arrive. Perhaps he can escape to Siberia, where he will eventually set up another empire, changing his name and his entire identity—starting over. He is dismayed that all his work, all his vision has come to nothing. Worse, he allowed himself to love Sylvia and believe that she cared for his daughter … but she blithely risked all their lives as part of her power games. Cold fury fills him.

Alex and Gregor feel as if they're being hunted. They hear cracking branches, see something moving. The reader may think it's another sabretooth or dire wolves—but instead, the wildman Psyk drops out of a tree, gripping his spear and brandishing his long hunting knife. He tackles Alex and raises his knife to kill the man.

Gregor has to drag his henchman off of Alex, yelling at him in English and Russian, before finally wrestling the knife away with main strength. Psyk is pumped up on the fern drug and not thinking clearly. At last, Gregor gets through to him—Alex is not the enemy. It was Senator Chesney.

Looking as if he has degenerated to a much more primitive human being, Psyk stalks off into the snowy forest without saying a word.

✦   ✦   ✦

When the sabretooths close in on the wrecked campsite, the Chinese businessman shoots twice more—but his aim is off each time.

Now Cassie races toward them on Zach's snowskimmer. Though she is herself bleeding from the dire wolf attack, Cassie yanks the magnum away from Hector Chu and stands in defense.

Within an hour, the sabretooths return, smelling blood. She recognizes one with a pronounced limp—the cat she knocked out of a tree during her survival trek back from the northern section of the Preserve. Feeling no compunctions now, Cassie kills the leader of the sabretooth pride. The other big cats run. The three humans are saved.

Senator Chesney is relieved at the rescue, but still annoyed that her carefully orchestrated, behind-the-scenes coup of the Resurrection Preserve has gone so clumsily wrong. She tells Cassie not to expect any gratitude, that Alex Pierce will still face charges, that all of the Resurrection work will be forfeit. She knows enough people in Washington that Alex, Cassie, and even his hotshot lawyer LeVay won't be able to stop her.

Astonishingly, a thick spear slams into Sylvia with such power that she doesn't even fall—it skewers her to a tree. She dies with the rant still on her lips.

On the other side of the campsite, Psyk stands silently, looking at what he has done. He thinks of his son, and all the crimes this woman committed for the sake of power, *civilized* crimes that never seem to warrant a proper punishment.

He walks into the forest, confident that he can always make more spears.

✦　　　✦　　　✦

Wrap up. With the blizzard abating, Alex and Gregor arrive back at the camp. Rescue operations are called in, the military standby troops, now no longer under the Senator's control.

Randall LeVay, though, has been able to scare up media copters as well, which fly over to see the mammoths that have been slaughtered by the Evos. The very idea of an illicit mammoth hunt by big-game hunters creates quite a scandal, and finally public sympathy turns. The participants are bound to face charges themselves. LeVay is sure he can tie everything up in the courts for years—certainly enough time for Alex to prove that his mammoths did not suffer from any sort of retrovirus, unlike the Japanese dwarf mammoths.

Finally Alex and Cassie are together. They are ready to face the scandal and challenges that will appear in the aftermath of the mammoth hunt. It will not be easy. But they are proud of what they have accomplished in their lives, proud of what they have found in each other.

Cassie reveals that she has found the preserved genetic samples of Helen (and saved them from the Evo attack). She is afraid to know what Alex intended to do with them—did he mean to try to clone his dead wife? Heartsick, but healing, Alex reveals that Helen was *pregnant* when she was killed in Montana; he had hoped one day to have another child with a surrogate mother, because at the time he had never imagined he could love again. Now, though, he has changed his mind.

Many of the Preserve's animals will have already escaped into the Arctic wilderness, since the fences are now down—both the sonic fences around the

Resurrection Preserve, and the ones around Alex Pierce's heart....

We see Psyk alone, trudging farther north, into the wilderness. He has a new spear, his knife, and a few tools. It is all he needs. He sees himself as a great hunter, returning to the old ways, the old life, and is content with the prospect.

Gregor manages to slip away, picked up by his backup team. "One always has a bolt-hole," he says as he leaves Alex.

He has easily bribed his way out of Alaska and is now hurrying to the Siberian mainland. There he will create a new identity for himself, find the stashes of wealth he has hidden, call in a few old favors, and start all over again.

In a bittersweet "sense-of-wonder" final scene, Gregor is flying low on his way back to Russia, to put his life back together. As he cruises over the Bering Strait, Gregor looks down. He sees the dark shapes of woolly mammoths, free and healthy and escaped from the Resurrection Preserve, swimming across the icy waters toward the vast, virgin wastelands of Siberia....

BRINGING BACK THE MAMMOTHS

The notion of bringing vanished species back to life—"de-extinction"—hovers between reality and science fiction. It has sunk into the public mind over the past two decades, ever since *Jurassic Park* unleashed special-effects dinosaurs on the world.

Until the 2010s, the technology for de-extinction has lagged far behind the science fiction. Now we can see the prospect better, and several teams are working toward it.

But before looking into that, the big question is now not *could* we, but *should* we.

WHY?

Jurassic Park resurrected dinosaurs for their entertainment value. The disasters and excitement that followed were mostly due to bad management, not anything intrinsic to the idea. So any answer to the *why?* question has to start with what we can actually do.

Not dinosaurs, no. People forget that realistically, the only species we can hope to revive now are those that died within the past few tens of thousands of years. Only for those can we find remains that harbor intact cells or, at the very least, enough ancient DNA to reconstruct the creature's genome. Natural rates of decay mean that we can never have much hope of retrieving the full genome of *Tyrannosaurus rex*, which vanished about 65 million years ago. Any species theoretically capable of being revived all disappeared within our reign, while humanity rapidly climbed toward world domination. And ever faster, we humans were the culprits who wiped them out—by hunting, destroying habitats, or spreading diseases.

This fact frames the major argument for bringing them back.

Michael Archer, a paleontologist at the University of New South Wales, who has championed de-extinction for years, puts it thus: "If we're talking about species we drove extinct, then I think we have an obligation to try to do this." Any system of justice dictates that if damage can be restored, it should be, by the perpetrator.

Of course, some say that reviving a species that no longer exists amounts to playing God. Archer scoffs at the notion. "I think we played God when we exterminated these animals."

Another objection is more detailed. "Mammoths, like elephants, were intelligent, highly social animals," says Adrian Lister, paleontologist and mammoth expert at the Natural History Museum in London. "Cloning would give you a single animal, which would live all alone in a park, a zoo, or a lab—not in its native habitat, which no longer exists. You're basically creating a curio."

But of course, raising not one but a herd of mammoths would mean they could forage on their own, closely watched by humans, who can help with their reintroduction. Tom Gilbert, an expert in ancient DNA at Copenhagen University (who has pioneered the harvesting of mammoth DNA from hair) thinks that this is reasonable. Indeed, he admits that as a student of mammoths, he'd be the first to go see one trundle across a paddock. But he does question both the utility and the wisdom of cloning extinct species. "If you can do a mammoth, you can do anything else that's dead, including your grandmother. But in a world in global warming and with limited resources for research, do you really want to bring back your dead grandmother?"

That pseudo-grandmother would not have the memories of yours, of course—she would be a child. The essence of "grandmotherness" is surely the intelligence and social connections we associate with our grandmothers. With mammoths, it's their sheer majesty.

There are many extinct creatures that some would bring back: the dodo and the great auk, the Tasmanian tiger and the Chinese river dolphin, the passenger pigeon (which only a century or so ago numbered in hundreds of millions in America). They are from a long list of animals humans have driven extinct, sometimes deliberately. And with many more species now endangered, they will have much more company in the years to come.

There's another large issue, too. Once species resurrections seem near, we would have to prepare habitats for them, perhaps ones that don't exist now. Also, we would not allow hunting of a recovered species, at least until they had a large population. (Thinking on how to fund all the work to resurrect mammoths, imagine how much the rich would pay to go on a mammoth hunt!) For many species, though, there's no place left to call home.

The Chinese river dolphin became extinct due to pollution and other pressures from the human population on the Yangtze River. Things are just as bad there today. Around the world, frogs are getting decimated by a human-spread pathogen called the chytrid fungus. If Australian biologists someday release a resurrected version of the rare gastric brooding frogs into their old mountain streams, they would promptly become extinct again. Fixing the habitat has to come first.

"Without an environment to put re-created species back into, the whole exercise is futile and a gross waste of money," says Glenn Albrecht, director of the Institute for Social Sustainability at Murdoch University in Australia.

In this sense, mammoths have an edge. There is plenty of Arctic tundra for them to rove. Indeed, trees, and shrubs are spreading north as global climate change warms the Arctic, so there will be more of that fodder for mammoths.

Still, even if species resurrection were a complete logistical success, the questions would not end. Take passenger pigeons, famously wiped out by hunting in the 19th Century. Brought back, they might find the rebounding forests of the eastern United States a welcoming home.

Some would cry, "But wouldn't that be, in effect, the introduction of a genetically engineered organism into the environment?" Yes, but that's not new. We've done it with many plants and several animals already. Plus, "genetically engineered organism" is a buzzword that neglects how we have for thousands of years turned natural species into forms more useful to us—through breeding, or "animal husbandry." (Notice how that term assumes that *we* are the husbands….)

Others say, "Could passenger pigeons become a reservoir for a virus that might wipe out another bird species? And how would the residents of Chicago, New York, or Washington, D.C., feel about a new pigeon species arriving in their cities, darkening their skies, and covering their streets with snowstorms of dung?" These seem to me minor issues, especially since viruses evolve naturally all around us, all the time. And cities clean their streets often, anyway. A study of modern cities showed that they were cleaner than in the 19th Century, since horses drop a lot of dung.

There are other arguments, too. "There is clearly a terrible urgency to saving threatened species and habitats," says John Wiens, an evolutionary biologist at Stony Brook University in New York. "As far as I can see, there is little urgency for bringing back extinct ones. Why invest millions of dollars in bringing a handful of species back from the dead, when there are millions still waiting to be discovered, described, and protected?"

An answer to that is, okay, let people do it with private investment, not public research funds. Charities can help. Once you have a living mammoth, the social momentum will build. Millions will pay to see them.

But does that mean we *should* bring any species back? Would the world be that much richer for having, say, an extinct kind of female frog that grows little frogs in their stomachs? There might be tangible benefits, such as the insights the frogs might be able to provide about reproduction, from their return. Such insights might someday lead to treatments for pregnant women who have trouble carrying babies to term.

Mammoths are a special, striking case—we probably killed them off, so they're our problem. Still, for many scientists, de-extinction is a distraction from the pressing work required to stave off mass extinctions. De-extinction advocates counter that the cloning and genomic engineering technologies being developed for de-extinction could also help preserve endangered species, especially ones that don't breed easily in captivity. And though cutting-edge biotechnology can be expensive when it's first developed, it could become very cheap very quickly. "Maybe some people thought polio vaccines were a distraction from iron lungs," says George Church of Harvard. "It's hard in advance to say what's distraction and what's salvation."

But what would we be willing to call salvation? Even if Church and his colleagues manage to retrofit every passenger pigeon-specific trait into a rock pigeon, say, would the resulting creature truly be a passenger pigeon or just an engineered curiosity? If some do produce a single gastric brooding frog, does that mean they've revived the species? If that frog doesn't have a mate, then it becomes an amphibian version of Celia, and its species is as good as extinct. Would it be enough to keep a population of the frogs in a lab or perhaps in a zoo, where people could gawk at it? Or would it need to be introduced back into the wild to be truly de-extinct?

"The history of putting species back after they've gone extinct in the wild is fraught with difficulty," says conservation biologist Stuart Pimm of Duke University.

A huge effort went into restoring the Arabian oryx to the wild, for example. But after the animals were returned to a refuge in central Oman in 1982, poachers wiped almost all of them out. "We had the animals, and we put them back, and the world wasn't ready," says Pimm. "Having the species solves only a tiny, tiny part of the problem."

Critics admonish that the introduction of a now-alien mammoth species could damage the fragile ecosystem of the existing tundra. To this criticism Russian scientist Sergey Zimov replied: "Tundra—that is not an eco-system. Such systems had not existed on the planet [before the disappearance of the big creatures, the megafauna], and there is nothing to cherish in the tundra. Of course, it would be silly to create a desert instead of the tundra, but if the same site would evolve into a steppe, then it certainly would improve the environment. If deer, foxes, bovines were more abundant, nature would only benefit from this. And people too. However, the danger still exists, of course, you have to be very careful. If it is a revival of the steppes, then, for example, small animals are really dangerous to release without control. As for large herbivores—no danger, as they are very easy to remove again."

De-extinction advocates are pondering these questions, and most believe they need to be resolved before any major project moves forward. Hank Greely, a leading bioethicist at Stanford University, has taken a keen interest in investigating the ethical and legal implications of de-extinction. And yet for Greely, as for many others, the very fact that science has advanced to the point that such a spectacular feat is possible is a compelling reason to embrace de-extinction, not to shun it.

"What intrigues me is just that it's really cool," Greely says. "A saber-toothed cat? It would be neat to see one of those."

How?

An analogy: the DNA library. For the mammoth carcasses we've found, we have many copies of the same book—DNA segments—but each copy has only a page or two left in it. Worse, the pages weren't numbered. In each case, the blind rub of millennia had ripped out all but a few of the genetic plans.

The trick lies in realizing that each fragment of DNA found was a book with different pages left. Find enough books, compare the pages, stitch and splice and edit … and eventually patch together a complete book.

After all the talk about molecular groups and amino acids, the library analogy *feels* right. Even a congressman can grasp it.

For decades now, biologists have been finding suitable DNA in frozen mammoth bodies. The next step is to recover and, if possible, combine the DNA with similar living animals such as the Asian elephant, closest living relative to mammoths. If scientists can implant a reconstructed mammoth egg, using advanced cloning techniques, an elephant may give birth to some mammoth-related or true mammoth species.

That lies probably decades away. But we can prepare for it in worked-out, useful ways. A consensus has emerged by 2015: De-extinction is now within reach. "It's gone very much further, very much more rapidly than anyone ever would've imagined," says Ross

MacPhee, a curator of mammalogy at the American Museum of Natural History in New York.

Some scientists are tackling a less daunting challenge: cloning endangered or very recently extinct animals. The San Diego Zoo and the Audubon Center for Research of Endangered Species in New Orleans both maintain "frozen zoos," where the DNA of a growing number of endangered species is stored in tanks of liquid nitrogen at –320°F.

In 2003, scientists at Advanced Cell Technology used cells stored at the San Diego facility to successfully clone across the species barrier. They created two bantengs, an endangered Southeast Asian ox, by inserting banteng DNA into domestic cow eggs and placing the resulting embryos in ordinary cows as foster-mothers. It worked.

There is talk of using similar methods to clone endangered giant pandas, African bongo antelopes, and Sumatran tigers. Ultimately scientists hope to re-create extinct species like the Pyrenean ibex and the thylacine, or Tasmanian tiger. (The "tiger" is actually a dog. It's the largest known meat-eating marsupial of modern times. It was a relatively shy, nocturnal creature with the general appearance of a medium-to-large-size dog, except for its stiff tail. The last one in captivity died in 1939.)

The journal *Scientific American* in an editorial con-demning de-extinction, pointed out that the technologies involved could have secondary applications, specifically to help species on the verge of extinction regain their genetic diversity, for example the black-footed ferret or the northern white rhino. *Scientific American* thought, though, that such research "should be conducted under the mantle of preserving modern biodiversity rather than conjuring extinct species from the grave."

Of course, a resurrected species, while being genetically the same as previously living specimens, will not have the same behavior as the real, extinct, thing. The first animal to be brought back will be raised by parents of a different species (the fetus's host), not the one that died out. So it will have differing mothering techniques and other behaviors we cannot know.

For decades, explorers and scientists have pulled woolly mammoth carcasses from the Siberian tundra and Canada. These preserved soft-tissue remains and DNA of woolly mammoths make possible two methods:

- ***First Method:*** Cloning, which would involve removal of the DNA-containing the nucleus of an egg cell from a female elephant. Then replace with a nucleus from woolly mammoth tissue. Stimulate that cell into dividing, insert back into the female elephant. The resulting mammoth/elephant calf would have the genes of the woolly mammoth, though its fetal environment would be different. So far, even the most intact mammoths have had little usable DNA because they have degraded in time. There is not yet enough to guide the production of an embryo.

But the egg would have to be definitely complete. The best method of cloning a mammoth, or any other extinct animal, is to recover its complete DNA sequence. For mammoths, the strand is estimated to be more than 4.5 billion base pairs long—and to express this data in flesh and blood.

In 2009 a group at Pennsylvania State University, led by Webb Miller and Stephan C. Schuster, published 70 percent of the mammoth genome, laying out much of the basic data that might be required to make a mammoth.

This publication is a good start. Still, the remaining 30 percent of the genome would have to be recovered and the entire genome resequenced several more times to weed out errors that have crept into the ancient DNA over the centuries as it degraded. Scientists would also have to package the DNA into chromosomes—and at present they don't even know how many chromosomes the mammoth had. Yet none of these tasks appears insurmountable, especially in light of recent technical advances, such as a new generation of high-speed sequencers and a simple, inexpensive technique for recovering high-quality DNA from mammoth hair. "It's a simple question of time and money, not of technology anymore," says Schuster.

Here's where the African and Asian elephants may be vital. They are the mammoth's closest relatives in the saga of evolution.

The Penn State team used the African elephant genome as a guide to reassemble the pieces of mammoth DNA they'd recovered from hair samples. But this ancient DNA is far too fragmented to use to create an organism. So one way to make living mammoth genetic material might be to modify elephant chromosomes at each of the estimated 400,000 sites where they differ from the mammoth's—effectively, rewriting an elephant's cells into a mammoth's. If researchers can figure out how mammoth DNA was organized into chromosomes, another strategy would be to synthesize the entire genome from scratch, although so far the largest genome to be synthesized was only a thousandth the size of the mammoth's.

Once scientists have functional mammoth chromosomes in hand, they could wrap them in a membrane to create an artificial cell nucleus. Then they could follow the approach pioneered in creating Dolly, the sheep cloned in 1996 by scientists at the Roslin Institute in Scotland: Remove the nucleus of an elephant's egg. Replace it with the rebuilt mammoth nucleus. Electrically stimulate the egg to trigger initial cell division into an embryo. Eventually, transfer the embryo into an elephant's womb for gestation. Each of these steps has significant question marks. No one knows, for example, just how to build a mammoth nucleus. Harvesting an elephant egg is difficult, and bringing a mammoth fetus to term in an elephant uterus is fraught with uncertainties.

Still, this method may be the best bet. At least it's systematic.

* ***Second Method:*** Similar to the first method, but relies on good luck—finding an intact mammoth sperm cell. Take sperm cells from a frozen woolly mammoth carcass. Inject them into an elephant egg cell. The offspring would be an elephant-mammoth hybrid. Repeat, so more hybrids could be used in breeding. Use skills of animal husbandry to ferret out the more mammoth-like hybrids. After several generations of crossbreeding, these hybrids can converge toward an almost pure woolly mammoth. Such bred hybrids could gain notable adaptations. The mammoth genes contain instructions on adaptations to a much colder environment than modern day elephants. Geneticists are currently doing this at Harvard. They have already successfully made changes in the elephant genome with the genes that gave the woolly mammoth its cold-resistance blood, longer hair, and extra layer of fat.

There are problems, of course. Sperm cells of modern mammals remain potent for 15 years, at most, after deep-freezing. Whether mammoth sperm can be viable is unknown. That makes this method iffy.

But early work has begun. An experiment with an Asian elephant and an African elephant produced a live calf, but it died of defects at less than two weeks old. In 2008, a Japanese team found usable DNA in the brains of mice that had been frozen for 16 years. They hope to use similar methods to find usable mammoth DNA. In 2011, Japanese scientists announced plans to clone mammoths within six years.

In 2009 the first extinct animal was cloned back to life—an Iberian wild goat. The clone lived for only seven minutes before dying of lung defects. Efforts continue. The woolly mammoth genome has been mapped, and a complete strand of DNA may be synthesized soon. However, it was reported in March 2014 that blood recovered from a frozen mammoth carcass in 2013 now gives scientists a "high chance" of cloning the woolly mammoth, despite previous troubles.

Ecological work is moving forward, too. A revived woolly mammoth or mammoth-elephant hybrid might find suitable habitat in the tundra and taiga forest ecozones of the Arctic. They may also find refuge in a Pleistocene Park, an experiment by Russian scientist Sergey Zimov. He aims to recreate the mammoth steppe, the woolly mammoth's former habitat. Indeed, mammoths could recreate the steppe, since they are highly effective in quickly clearing brush and forest, by stripping them away and eating them. That will let grasses colonize the area. No modern arctic large animals can do that.

WHEN?

Given the great advances since the "genetics revolution" of the 1990s, resurrection seems near.

"I laughed when Steven Spielberg said that cloning extinct animals was inevitable," says Hendrik Poinar of McMaster University, an authority on ancient DNA who served as a scientific consultant for a film about the making of *Jurassic Park*. "But I'm not laughing anymore, at least about mammoths. This is going to happen. It's just a matter of working out the details."

Yes, but for how long?

The first method above will take a decade at least, I believe. Maybe two.

The second relies on luck. Several teams are steadily recovering mammoth carcasses across Siberia. If they can find a viable sperm cell, this would be the way to go. It could yield a mammoth in a decade.

So, some hope?

The array of scientists from major institutions that I've cited here gives voice to a rising chorus of such adventurers. That such scientists are willing to devote endless hours to this quest—and get funding!—is the most positive aspect of the entire mammoth issue.

To be sure, as the prospect draws nearer, we will see opponents. There always are. Our story "Mammoth Dawn" depicts this.

My money, though, is on the mammoth resurrectionists. They are aided by parallel work from those seeking to bring back the great auk, the Tasmanian tiger, the passenger pigeon. They seek a grander future with more possibilities in it—and not, like many technologies, just for humans.

—Gregory Benford

About the Authors

KEVIN J. ANDERSON has published 130 books, 54 of which have been national or international bestsellers. He has over 23 million copies in print in thirty languages. He is best known for writing numerous novels in the Star Wars, X-Files, and Dune universes, as well as a steampunk fantasy novel, *Clockwork Angels*, with legendary rock group Rush.

His original works include the Saga of Seven Suns series, the Terra Incognita fantasy trilogy, the Saga of Shadows trilogy, and his humorous horror series featuring Dan Shamble, Zombie PI.

He has written comics for DC, Marvel, IDW, Topps, BOOM!, and Wildstorm. He edited numerous anthologies, including the *Five by Five* and *Blood Lite* series. He produced two rock albums from the super-group Roswell Six, featuring stars from legendary groups Kansas, Dream Theater, Saga and Asia, with lyrics written together with his wife Rebecca Moesta. He and Rebecca are the publishers of WordFire Press, with over 200 titles in print and eBook format, from 35 different authors.

Kevin has climbed all 54 mountain peaks in Colorado over 14,000 ft and he just completed hiking the 500 miles of the Colorado Trail. And he also enjoys Colorado microbrews.

GREGORY BENFORD has published over forty books, mostly novels. Nearly all remain in print, some after a quarter of a century. His fiction has won many awards, including the Nebula Award for his novel *Timescape*. A winner of the United Nations Medal for Literature, he is a professor of physics at the University of California, Irvine. He is a Woodrow Wilson Fellow, was Visiting Fellow at Cambridge University, and in 1995 received the Lord Prize for contributions to science. He won the Japan Seiun Award for Dramatic Presentation with his 7-hour series, A Galactic Odyssey. In 2007 he won the Asimov Award for science writing. In 2006 he co-founded Genescient, a biotech company devoted to extending human longevity.

His 1999 analysis of what endures, *Deep Time: How Humanity Communicates Across Millennia*, has been widely read. A fellow of the American Physical Society and a member of the World Academy of Arts and Sciences, he continues his research in both astrophysics and plasma physics and biotech. Time allowing, he continues to write both fiction and nonfiction.

If You Liked ...

If you liked *Mammoth Dawn*, you might also enjoy:

The Dark Lady
by Mike Resnick

Climbing Olympus
by Kevin J. Anderson

Blindfold
by Kevin J. Anderson

Other WordFire Press Titles

Our list of other WordFire Press authors and titles is always growing. To find out more and to see our selection of titles, visit us at:

wordfirepress.com